'Saki' (H. H. Munro) was born in Burma in 1870 and brought up under the strict tutelage of his aunt and grandmother in North Devon. He joined the Burma Police in 1893 but resigned because of ill-health and came to London to write. He first became known for his fanciful Tory political sketches in the *Westminster Graphic* and from 1902 to 1908 he was a correspondent for the *Morning Post* in Paris, Poland and Russia. He published two novels, *The Unbearable Bassington* (1912) and the pro-war fantasy *When William Came* (1913). He was best known for his volumes of short stories such as *Reginald* (1904), *Reginald in Russia* (1910), *The Chronicles of Clovis* (1911) and *Beasts and Super Beasts* (1914). He enlisted in 1914, refused a commission and was killed in France in 1916.

THE CHRONICLES OF CLOVIS

BY
'SAKI'
(H. H. Munro)

With an Introduction by
Auberon Waugh

Penguin Books

PENGUIN BOOKS

Published by the Penguin Group
27 Wrights Lane, London W8 5TZ, England
Viking Penguin Inc., 40 West 23rd Street, New York, New York 10010, USA
Penguin Books Australia Ltd, Ringwood, Victoria, Australia
Penguin Books Canada Ltd, 2801 John Street, Markham, Ontario, Canada L3R 1B4
Penguin Books (NZ) Ltd, 182–190 Wairau Road, Auckland 10, New Zealand

Penguin Books Ltd, Registered Offices: Harmondsworth, Middlesex, England

First published 1911
Published in Penguin Books 1948
Reissued with an Introduction 1986
3 5 7 9 10 8 6 4 2

Printed and bound in Great Britain by
Cox & Wyman Ltd, Reading

To the Lynx Kitten, with his reluctantly given consent,
this book is affectionately dedicated
H. H. M. *August, 1922*

CONTENTS

INTRODUCTION   vii

ESMÉ   7

THE MATCH-MAKER   13

TOBERMORY   16

MRS. PACKLETIDE'S TIGER   25

THE STAMPEDING OF LADY BASTABLE   29

THE BACKGROUND   33

HERMAN THE IRASCIBLE——A STORY OF THE
        GREAT WEEP   37

THE UNREST-CURE   40

THE JESTING OF ARLINGTON STRINGHAM   47

SREDNI VASHTAR   51

ADRIAN   57

THE CHAPLET   62

THE QUEST   66

WRATISLAV   71

THE EASTER EGG   75

FILBOID STUDGE, THE STORY OF A MOUSE
        THAT HELPED   80

THE MUSIC ON THE HILL   84

THE STORY OF ST. VESPALUUS   91

THE WAY TO THE DAIRY   100

THE PEACE OFFERING   108

CONTENTS

THE PEACE of MOWSLE BARTON   114

THE TALKING-OUT OF TARRINGTON   122

THE HOUNDS OF FATE   125

THE RECESSIONAL   133

A MATTER OF SENTIMENT   138

THE SECRET SIN OF SEPTIMUS BROPE   143

'MINISTERS OF GRACE'   152

THE REMOULDING OF GROBY LINGTON   163

INTRODUCTION

HECTOR MUNRO, whose pen-name Saki is thought to derive from the golden boy or catamite of that name in FitzGerald's *Rubáiyát*, remains a strangely mysterious figure. His sister, Ethel, destroyed all his papers after his death in the fighting of November 1916 near Beaumont-Hamel. Although the bare outlines of his life are well known, it has been remarked that his memory survives in practically none of the writings of his contemporaries. His cousin Major C. W. Mercer (better known as Dornford Yates, the novelist) wrote a brief memoir testifying to Munro's cheerfulness and charm, but Mercer was fifteen years younger and saw him only a few times. The chief primary source appears to be the brief memoir written by his sister which appeared with a post-humously published volume of Saki's work, *The Square Egg*, in 1924. Her evidence is thought to be tainted by a secretive-ness about her brother which bordered on obsession. Although Ethel laid down the guidelines for all subsequent speculation, revealing the existence of two draconian aunts in Devon, Munro's own writings about these aunts do not entirely support her picture of them and it seems possible that his attitude to women was determined even more by the presence of this difficult – if not slightly deranged – sister, who became his responsibility after their father died in 1907. All the evidence suggests that Munro was a person of charm, wit and social ease, never happier than when playing bridge at his beloved Cocoa Tree Club. There may be no significance in the fact that he seems to have chosen rather dim company to enchant.

The bare facts, as I say, are well known. Hector Hugh Munro was born in Akyab, Burma, the third of three children in the family of an Inspector General of the Burma Police. Before he was two years old his mother had died and all three children were sent to live in Devon with their grandmother and two aunts, Charlotte ('Tom') and Augusta. Tom was the older by fifteen years. According to Ethel's account, the two aunts were sworn enemies, both of them immensely powerful characters. P. G. Wodehouse had exactly the same experience of being brought up by overpowering aunts eleven years later. He, too, was sent home from the rigours of colonial life, and the experience seems to have had a similar effect on his imaginative development, except that Wodehouse's writing is entirely devoid of hatred or cruelty. He would never have sent one of his aunts to be eaten by a pole-cat ferret, as Saki apparently consigned his Aunt Augusta in *Sredni Vashtar*. The boy in that story is dying – an odd, dramatically unnecessary touch – and we are given to understand that he is dying because his imaginative life is being stifled by the pestering boredom and domination of his terrible female guardian.

Here there seems to be evidence of consuming hatred and resentment. Yet the three children – Charles, the older brother, later became governor of Mountjoy Prison, Dublin – plainly had a richly imaginative childhood. I suspect that Munro's frustration and impatience with women had other roots, and that he agreed to transfer them to his two aunts in deference to the wishes of the sister who survived them all.

After leaving Bedford Grammar School Munro lived happily with his father, by now retired from his service in the colonies, travelling abroad with him to Normandy, Germany, Austria and Davos Platz, in Switzerland, where he made friends with the tormented homosexual J. A. Symonds, thirty years his senior. Quite suddenly, at the age of twenty-three, he decided it was time he had a job, and set out to join the military police in Burma. After thirteen months of sickness and loneliness he returned to the bosom of his family in early 1895 and remained in Devon for two years before going to earn his living as a writer in London. In 1900 he published an immensely readable history of Russia, *The Rise of the Russian Empire*, now long out of print, and started a satirical column in the Liberal *Westminster Gazette*, describing the political scene in the manner of Lewis Carroll's *Alice in Wonderland*. It was judged a great success, although its follow-up, in the manner of Rudyard Kipling's *Just So Stories*, created less of an impression. But his politics were essentially Conservative, and it was with relief that he transferred to the *Morning Post* in 1902, serving as that newspaper's correspondent in the Balkans, in Warsaw and St Petersburg (which he adored) and Paris. When war broke out in August 1914 he was writing a column of political commentary in the magazine *Outlook*.

It was not until 1904, at the late age of thirty-three, that Saki's eventual direction began to emerge with the publication of the first Reginald book. Reginald is a cynical, flippant young man, like Clovis Sangrail and Comus Bassington, but these stories and sketches are still characterized by an adolescent glibness, which is a pale shadow of the High Camp that was to emerge in *Chronicles of Clovis* (1911).

In the second Reginald book, *Reginald in Russia* (1910), as the critic J. W. Lambert has observed, Saki struck all the notes within his creative range: the merely frivolous; the frivolous macabre; the rustic-horrific; the supernatural; the cynical; the melancholy-pessimistic; the merely melancholy. Again and again we find animals coming in as instruments of revenge for the folly of human beings. But Reginald seldom develops beyond the Wildean epigram, the adolescent desire to shock. Saki's driving ambition transcends the High Camp antics of his brilliant contemporary E. F. Benson (there is no evidence that the two ever met). It may or may not have been inspired by the hatreds and rage of the repressed homosexual – in the absence of evidence to the contrary, we must suppose that the homosexual side of his nature *was* repressed, as with E. F. Benson. Saki's main purpose, as I say, was to confront humanity with its odiousness, rather than with its absurdity.

This repressed homosexuality, if such it was, explains his rage with the Christian Church and his rage with women as restrictive, authoritarian figures. It also explains why his indulgence in primitive Greek–pagan mythological fantasies is not accompanied by any feeling of liberation. The god Pan, in Music on the Hill, is a vengeful, threatening deity. The golden, naked youth found disporting himself in an English woodland glade in *Gabriel-Ernst* turns out to be a werewolf. Nineteen-year-old Clovis, for all his beauty, charm and wit, is not a particularly amiable character, but he does not emerge as a figure of tragedy until his next incarnation, as Comus Bassington in *The Unbearable Bassington*. There the Reginald–Clovis–Bassington hero comes through as victim, the free spirit oppressed by a cruel world. Once that discovery was made, there was nothing left for the retarded adolescent Saki to do but get himself killed. To have lived into old age, like Norman Douglas and E. F. Benson, would have been to deny the validity of the short story as an art form.

Ethel Munro once suggested that her brother at one time wished to marry the daughter of a Devon landowner, but was prevented from doing so by lack of funds. I doubt the truth of this story. Lady Rosalind Northcote, a granddaughter of the Victorian politician Stafford Northcote, who was later made Earl of Iddesleigh, survived Munro by thirty-six years, dying unmarried in 1950. Such inquiries as I have been able to make about her do not suggest that she was the sort of woman who would have appealed to Hector Munro, the balletomane and friend of Nijinski whose misogyny runs clearly and unmistakably through nearly all his published work. Although his women are sometimes described as beautiful, I do not think that there is any suggestion anywhere that they are either desirable or pleasant.

The twenty-eight stories and short sketches in *The Chronicles of Clovis* show the full range of Saki's talent at a time when rage and indignation against humanity had not yet conquered the simple desire to please. Unless one can spot this rage, one might well mistake it for heartlessness or even vulgar snobbery. The fate of the 'gypsy brat' eaten by a hyena in *Esmé* is not, of course, intended to excite pity; but a feeling of outrage at the cruelty of fate and at the callousness of the participants complements, rather than denies, an appreciation of Saki's perverse humour. Tobermory, the speaking cat, immediately exposes the vanity and vice of human beings who have been patronizing him. Their reaction, to have him killed, is a perfect commentary on our normal response to un-welcome truth. Clovis's proposal to J. P. Huddle, the pillar of Anglican respectability, that his house should be used for a new, galvanizing form of Church witness – 'The Bishop is out for blood . . . We are going to massacre every Jew in the neighbourhood' – would not be funny at all if it were not for the absurdity and intellectual torpor of J. P. Huddle, thus exposed.

The same is true of Mrs Stringham's suicide in *The Jesting of Arlington Stringham*, where the idea that such a pompous man could possibly make a joke is so improbable that catastrophe must result. *Sredni Vashtar* reveals depths of misogyny which I have already explored, but *Adrian* reveals a more general misanthropy which might easily be mistaken for vulgar snob-bery. Like *The Quest*, which seems to express no more than the confirmed bachelor's hatred of children – with, perhaps, a hint of the homosexual's grudge against Christianity – it should be seen as showing the predicament of the imagin-ative, free and therefore superior man struggling to despise the hard world which rejects him. A free man cannot pay lip-service to the obvious untruth that the lower classes are de-lightful, babies are sweet.

This theme of the artist fighting desperately against a philis-tine world emerges again in *The Chaplet*, where the chef appears to have scored a temporary victory by drowning the bogus conductor in his soup, and in *Filboid Studge*, where the artist beats the philistines at their own game by inventing and marketing a new breakfast cereal but is then defeated by their ingratitude.

One could go on indefinitely relating Saki's stories to this version of his life-struggle. I am not sure how much it adds to the enjoyment of his wit, his perversity or his sparkling narrative inventiveness to relate them all to a speculative theory of this sort. But, in an age which sets enormous store by the quality of compassion, it might reduce the unease which Saki's apparent hard-heartedness often produces. Perhaps everybody should read *The Unbearable Bassington* before tackling this collection of stories. My theory that his apparent savagery is the result of emotional frustration may be a load of rubbish, but I feel it may do something to relieve the guilt of normally kind-hearted readers who find themselves enjoying these stories. If the modern age can see Saki's apparent cruelty as a lonely cry for pity and understanding I feel sure it will find his jokes more acceptable, and anything which spreads an appreciation of his excellent jokes must surely have a salutary effect on the modern world.

Auberon Waugh, 1985

ESME

'ALL hunting stories are the same,' said Clovis; 'just as all Turf stories are the same, and all——'

'My hunting story isn't a bit like any you've ever heard,' said the Baroness. 'It happened quite a while ago, when I was about twenty-three. I wasn't living apart from my husband then; you see, neither of us could afford to make the other a separate allowance. In spite of everything that proverbs may say, poverty keeps together more homes than it breaks up. But we always hunted with different packs. All this has nothing to do with the story.'

'We haven't arrived at the meet yet. I suppose there was a meet,' said Clovis.

'Of course there was a meet,' said the Baroness; 'all the usual crowd were there, especially Constance Broddle. Constance is one of those strapping florid girls that go so well with autumn scenery or Christmas decorations in church. "I feel a presentiment that something dreadful is going to happen," she said to me; "am I looking pale?"

'She was looking about as pale as a beetroot that has suddenly heard bad news.

'"You're looking nicer than usual," I said, "but that's so easy for you." Before she had got the right bearings of this remark we had settled down to business; hounds had found a fox lying out in some gorse-bushes.'

'I knew it,' said Clovis; 'in every fox-hunting story that I've ever heard there's been a fox and some gorse-bushes.'

'Constance and I were well mounted,' continued the Baroness serenely, 'and we had no difficulty in keeping ourselves in the first flight, though it was a fairly stiff run. Towards the finish, however, we must have held rather too independent a line, for we lost the hounds, and found ourselves plodding aimlessly along miles away from anywhere. It was fairly exasperating,

7

and my temper was beginning to let itself go by inches, when on pushing our way through an accommodating hedge we were gladdened by the sight of hounds in full cry in a hollow just beneath us.

' " There they go," cried Constance, and then added in a gasp, " In Heaven's name, what are they hunting ? "

' It was certainly no mortal fox. It stood more than twice as high, had a short, ugly head, and an enormous thick neck.

' " It's a hyæna," I cried ; " it must have escaped from Lord Pabham's Park."

' At that moment the hunted beast turned and faced its pursuers, and the hounds (there were only about six couple of them) stood round in a half-circle and looked foolish. Evidently they had broken away from the rest of the pack on the trail of this alien scent, and were not quite sure how to treat their quarry now they had got him.

' The hyæna hailed our approach with unmistakable relief and demonstrations of friendliness. It had probably been accustomed to uniform kindness from humans, while its first experience of a pack of hounds had left a bad impression. The hounds looked more than ever embarrassed as their quarry paraded its sudden intimacy with us, and the faint toot of a horn in the distance was seized on as a welcome signal for unobtrusive departure. Constance and I and the hyæna were left alone in the gathering twilight.

' " What are we to do ? " asked Constance.

' " What a person you are for questions," I said.

' " Well, we can't stay here all night with a hyæna," she retorted.

' " I don't know what your ideas of comfort are," I said ; " but I shouldn't think of staying here all night even without a hyæna. My home may be an unhappy one, but at least it has hot and cold water laid on, and domestic service, and other conveniences which we shouldn't find here. We had better make for that ridge of trees to the right ; I imagine the Crowley road is just beyond."

'We trotted off slowly along a faintly marked cart-track, with the beast following cheerfully at our heels.

'"What on earth are we to do with the hyæna?" came the inevitable question.

'"What does one generally do with hyænas?" I asked crossly.

'"I've never had anything to do with one before," said Constance.

'"Well, neither have I. If we even knew its sex we might give it a name. Perhaps we might call it Esmé. That would do in either case."

'There was still sufficient daylight for us to distinguish wayside objects, and our listless spirits gave an upward perk as we came upon a small half-naked gipsy brat picking blackberries from a low-growing bush. The sudden apparition of two horse-women and a hyæna set it off crying, and in any case we should scarcely have gleaned any useful geographical information from that source; but there was a probability that we might strike a gipsy encampment somewhere along our route. We rode on hopefully but uneventfully for another mile or so.

'"I wonder what that child was doing there," said Constance presently.

'"Picking blackberries. Obviously."

'"I don't like the way it cried," pursued Constance; "somehow its wail keeps ringing in my ears."

'I did not chide Constance for her morbid fancies; as a matter of fact the same sensation, of being pursued by a persistent fretful wail, had been forcing itself on my rather over-tired nerves. For company's sake I hulloed to Esmé, who had lagged somewhat behind. With a few springy bounds he drew up level, and then shot past us.

'The wailing accompaniment was explained. The gipsy child was firmly, and I expect painfully, held in his jaws.

'"Merciful Heaven!" screamed Constance, "what on earth shall we do? What are we to do?"

'I am perfectly certain that at the Last Judgment Constance will ask more questions than any of the examining Seraphs.

' " Can't we do something ? " she persisted tearfully, as Esmé cantered easily along in front of our tired horses.

' Personally I was doing everything that occurred to me at the moment. I stormed and scolded and coaxed in English and French and gamekeeper language; I made absurd, ineffectual cuts in the air with my thongless hunting-crop; I hurled my sandwich case at the brute; in fact, I really don't know what more I could have done. And still we lumbered on through the deepening dusk, with that dark uncouth shape lumbering ahead of us, and a drone of lugubrious music floating in our ears. Suddenly Esmé bounded aside into some thick bushes, where we could not follow; the wail rose to a shriek and then stopped altogether. This part of the story I always hurry over, because it is really rather horrible. When the beast joined us again, after an absence of a few minutes, there was an air of patient understanding about him, as though he knew that he had done something of which we disapproved, but which he felt to be thoroughly justifiable.

' " How can you let that ravening beast trot by your side ? " asked Constance. She was looking more than ever like an albino beetroot.

' " In the first place, I can't prevent it," I said; " and in the second place, whatever else he may be, I doubt if he's ravening at the present moment."

' Constance shuddered. " Do you think the poor little thing suffered much ? " came another of her futile questions.

' " The indications were all that way," I said; " on the other hand, of course, it may have been crying from sheer temper. Children sometimes do."

' It was nearly pitch-dark when we emerged suddenly into the high road. A flash of lights and the whir of a motor went past us at the same moment at uncomfortably close quarters. A thud and a sharp screeching yell followed a second later. The car drew up, and when I had ridden back to the spot I found a young man bending over a dark motionless mass lying by the roadside.

' " You have killed my Esmé," I exclaimed bitterly.

' " I'm so awfully sorry," said the young man; " I keep dogs myself, so I know what you must feel about it. I'll do anythink I can in reparation."

' " Please bury him at once," I said; " that much I think I may ask of you."

' " Bring the spade, William," he called to the chauffeur. Evidently hasty roadside interments were contingencies that had been provided against.

' The digging of a sufficiently large grave took some little time. " I say, what a magnificent fellow," said the motorist as the corpse was rolled over into the trench. " I'm afraid he must have been rather a valuable animal."

' " He took second in the puppy class at Birmingham last year," I said resolutely.

' Constance snorted loudly.

' " Don't cry, dear," I said brokenly; " it was all over in a moment. He couldn't have suffered much."

' " Look here," said the young fellow desperately, " you simply must let me do something by way of reparation."

' I refused sweetly, but as he persisted I let him have my address.

' Of course, we kept our own counsel as to the earlier episodes of the evening. Lord Pabham never advertised the loss of his hyæna; when a strictly fruit-eating animal strayed from his park a year or two previously he was called upon to give compensation in eleven cases of sheep-worrying and practically to re-stock his neighbours' poultry-yards, and an escaped hyæna would have mounted up to something on the scale of a Government grant. The gipsies were equally unobtrusive over their missing offspring; I don't suppose in large encampments they really know to a child or two how many they've got.' .

The Baroness paused reflectively, and then continued:

' There was a sequel to the adventure, though. I got

through the post a charming little diamond brooch, with the name Esmé set in a sprig of rosemary. Incidentally, too, I lost the friendship of Constance Broddle. You see, when I sold the brooch I quite properly refused to give her any share of the proceeds. I pointed out that the Esmé part of the affair was my own invention, and the hyæna part of it belonged to Lord Pabham, if it really was his hyæna, of which, of course, I've no proof.'

THE MATCH-MAKER

THE grill-room clock struck eleven with the respectful un-obtrusiveness of one whose mission in life is to be ignored. When the flight of time should really have rendered abstinence and migration imperative the lighting apparatus would signal the fact in the usual way.

Six minutes later Clovis approached the supper-table, in the blessed expectancy of one who has dined sketchily and long ago.

' I'm starving,' he announced, making an effort to sit down gracefully and read the menu at the same time.

' So I gathered,' said his host, ' from the fact that you were nearly punctual.   I ought to have told you that I'm a Food Reformer.   I've ordered two bowls of bread-and-milk and some health biscuits.   I hope you don't mind.'

Clovis pretended afterwards that he didn't go white above the collar-line for the fraction of a second.

' All the same,' he said, ' you ought not to joke about such things.   There really are such people.   I've known people who've met them.   To think of all the adorable things there are to eat in the world, and then to go through life munching sawdust and being proud of it.'

' They're like the Flagellants of the Middle Ages, who went about mortifying themselves.'

' They had some excuse,' said Clovis.   ' They did it to save their immortal souls, didn't they?   You needn't tell me that a man who doesn't love oysters and asparagus and good wines has got a soul, or a stomach either.   He's simply got the instinct for being unhappy highly developed.'

Clovis relapsed for a few golden moments into tender intimacies with a succession of rapidly disappearing oysters.

' I think oysters are more beautiful than any religion,' he resumed presently.   ' They not only forgive our unkindness to them; they justify it, they incite us to go on being perfectly horrid to them.   Once they arrive at the supper-table they seem to enter thoroughly into the spirit of the thing.   There's nothing in Christianity or Buddhism that quite matches the sympathetic unselfishness of an oyster.   Do you like my new waistcoat?   I'm wearing it for the first time to-night.'

'It looks like a great many others you've had lately, only worse.   New dinner waistcoats are becoming a habit with you.'

'They say one always pays for the excesses of one's youth; mercifully that isn't true about one's clothes.   My mother is thinking of getting married.'

'Again!'

'It's the first time.'

'Of course, you ought to know.   I was under the impression that she's been married once or twice at least.'

'Three times, to be mathematically exact.   I meant that it was the first time she'd thought about getting married; the other times she did it without thinking.   As a matter of fact, it's really I who am doing the thinking for her in this case. You see, it's quite two years since her last husband died.'

'You evidently think that brevity is the soul of widowhood.'

'Well, it struck me that she was getting moped, and beginning to settle down, which wouldn't suit her a bit.   The first symptom that I noticed was when she began to complain that we were living beyond our income.   All decent people live beyond their incomes nowadays, and those who aren't respectable live beyond other people's.   A few gifted individuals manage to do both.'

'It's hardly so much a gift as an industry.'

'The crisis came,' returned Clovis, 'when she suddenly started the theory that late hours were bad for one, and wanted me to be in by one o'clock every night.   Imagine that sort of thing for me, who was eighteen on my last birthday.'

'On your last two birthdays, to be mathematically exact.'

'Oh, well, that's not my fault.   I'm not going to arrive at nineteen as long as my mother remains at thirty-seven.   One must have some regard for appearances.'

'Perhaps your mother would age a little in the process of settling down.'

'That's the last thing she'd think of.   Feminine reformations always start in on the failings of other people.   That's why I was so keen on the husband idea.'

'Did you go as far as to select the gentleman, or did you merely throw out a general idea, and trust to the force of suggestion?'

'If one wants a thing done in a hurry one must see to it oneself.   I found a military Johnny hanging round on a loose end at the club, and took him home to lunch once or twice. He'd spent most of his life on the Indian frontier, building roads, and relieving famines and minimizing earthquakes, and all that sort of thing that one does do on frontiers.   He could talk sense to a peevish cobra in fifteen native languages, and probably knew what to do if you found a rogue elephant on your croquet-lawn; but he was shy and diffident with women. I told my mother privately that he was an absolute woman-hater; so, of course, she laid herself out to flirt all she knew, which isn't a little.'

'And was the gentleman responsive?'

'I hear he told some one at the club that he was looking out for a Colonial job, with plenty of hard work, for a young friend of his, so I gather that he has some idea of marrying into the family.'

'You seem destined to be the victim of the reformation, after all.'

Clovis wiped the trace of Turkish coffee and the beginnings of a smile from his lips, and slowly lowered his dexter eyelid. Which, being interpreted, probably meant, 'I *don't* think!'

TOBERMORY

IT was a chill, rain-washed afternoon of a late August day, that indefinite season when partridges are still in security or cold storage, and there is nothing to hunt—unless one is bounded on the north by the Bristol Channel, in which case one may lawfully gallop after fat red stags. Lady Blemley's house-party was not bounded on the north by the Bristol Channel, hence there was a full gathering of her guests round the tea-table on this particular afternoon. And, in spite of the blankness of the season and the triteness of the occasion, there was no trace in the company of that fatigued restlessness which means a dread of the pianola and a subdued hankering for auction bridge. The undisguised open-mouthed attention of the entire party was fixed on the homely negative personality of Mr. Cornelius Appin. Of all her guests, he was the one who had come to Lady Blemley with the vaguest reputation. Some one had said he was 'clever,' and he had got his invitation in the moderate expectation, on the part of his hostess, that some portion at least of his cleverness would be contributed to the general entertainment. Until tea-time that day she had been unable to discover in what direction, if any, his cleverness lay. He was neither a wit nor a croquet champion, a hypnotic force nor a begetter of amateur theatricals. Neither did his exterior suggest the sort of man in whom women are willing to pardon a generous measure of mental deficiency. He had subsided into mere Mr. Appin, and the Cornelius seemed a piece of transparent baptismal bluff. And now he was claiming to have launched on the world a discovery beside which the invention of gunpowder, of the printing-press, and of steam locomotion were inconsiderable trifles. Science had made bewildering strides in many directions during recent decades, but this thing seemed to belong to the domain of miracle rather than to scientific achievement.

'And do you really ask us to believe,' Sir Wilfrid was saying, 'that you have discovered a means for instructing animals in the art of human speech, and that dear old Tobermory has proved your first successful pupil?'

'It is a problem at which I have worked for the last seventeen years,' said Mr. Appin, 'but only during the last eight or nine months have I been rewarded with glimmerings of success. Of course I have experimented with thousands of animals, but latterly only with cats, those wonderful creatures which have assimilated themselves so marvellously with our civilization while retaining all their highly developed feral instincts. Here and there among cats one comes across an outstanding superior intellect, just as one does among the ruck of human beings, and when I made the acquaintance of Tobermory a week ago I saw at once that I was in contact with a " Beyond-cat " of extraordinary intelligence. I had gone far along the road to success in recent experiments; with Tobermory, as you call him, I have reached the goal."

Mr. Appin concluded his remarkable statement in a voice which he strove to divest of a triumphant inflection. No one said ' Rats,' though Clovis's lips moved in a monosyllabic contortion which probably invoked those rodents of disbelief.

'And do you mean to say,' asked Miss Resker, after a slight pause, ' that you have taught Tobermory to say and understand easy sentences of one syllable?"

'My dear Miss Resker,' said the wonder-worker patiently, 'one teaches little children and savages and backward adults in that piecemeal fashion; when one has once solved the problem of making a beginning with an animal of highly developed intelligence one has no need for those halting methods. Tobermory can speak our language with perfect correctness.'

This time Clovis very distinctly said, ' Beyond-rats!' Sir Wilfrid was more polite, but equally sceptical.

'Hadn't we better have the cat in and judge for ourselves?' suggested Lady Blemley.

Sir Wilfrid went in search of the animal, and the company settled themselves down to the languid expectation of witnessing some more or less adroit drawing-room ventriloquism.

In a minute Sir Wilfrid was back in the room, his face white beneath its tan and his eyes dilated with excitement.

' By Gad, it's true ! '

His agitation was unmistakably genuine, and his hearers started forward in a thrill of awakened interest.

Collapsing into an armchair he continued breathlessly: ' I found him dozing in the smoking-room, and called out to him to come for his tea.   He blinked at me in his usual way, and I said, " Come on, Toby; don't keep us waiting "; and, by Gad ! he drawled out in a most horribly natural voice that he'd come when he dashed well pleased !   I nearly jumped out of my skin ! '

Appin had preached to absolutely incredulous hearers; Sir Wilfrid's statement carried instant conviction.   A Babel-like chorus of startled exclamation arose, amid which the scientist sat mutely enjoying the first fruit of his stupendous discovery.

In the midst of the clamour Tobermory entered the room and made his way with velvet tread and studied unconcern across to the group seated round the tea-table.

A sudden hush of awkwardness and constraint fell on the company.   Somehow there seemed an element of embarrassment in addressing on equal terms a domestic cat of acknowledged dental ability.

' Will you have some milk, Tobermory ? ' asked Lady Blemley in a rather strained voice.

' I don't mind if I do,' was the response, couched in a tone of even indifference. A shiver of suppressed excitement went through the listeners, and Lady Blemley might be excused for pouring out the saucerful of milk rather unsteadily.

' I'm afraid I've spilt a good deal of it,' she said apologetically.

' After all, it's not my Axminster,' was Tobermory's rejoinder.

Another silence fell on the group, and then Miss Resker, in her best district-visitor manner, asked if the human language had been difficult to learn.   Tobermory looked squarely at her for a moment and then fixed his gaze serenely on the middle distance.   It was obvious that boring questions lay outside his scheme of life.

'What do you think of human intelligence?' asked Mavis Pellington lamely.

'Of whose intelligence in particular?' asked Tobermory coldly.

'Oh, well, mine for instance,' said Mavis, with a feeble laugh.

'You put me in an embarrassing position,' said Tobermory, whose tone and attitude certainly did not suggest a shred of embarrassment.   'When your inclusion in this house-party was suggested Sir Wilfrid protested that you were the most brainless woman of his acquaintance, and that there was a wide distinction between hospitality and the care of the feeble-minded.   Lady Blemley replied that your lack of brain-power was the precise quality which had earned you your invitation, as you were the only person she could think of who might be idiotic enough to buy their old car.   You know, the one they call " The Envy of Sisyphus," because it goes quite nicely up-hill if you push it.'

Lady Blemley's protestations would have had greater effect if she had not casually suggested to Mavis only that morning that the car in question would be just the thing for her down at her Devonshire home.

Major Barfield plunged in heavily to effect a diversion.

'How about your carryings-on with the tortoiseshell puss up at the stables, eh?'

The moment he had said it every one realized the blunder.

'One does not usually discuss these matters in public,' said Tobermory frigidly.   'From a slight observation of your ways since you've been in this house I should imagine you'd find it inconvenient if I were to shift the conversation on to your own little affairs.'

The panic which ensued was not confined to the Major.

'Would you like to go and see if cook has got your dinner ready?' suggested Lady Blemley hurriedly, affecting to ignore the fact that it wanted at least two hours to Tobermory's dinner-time.

'Thanks,' said Tobermory, 'not quite so soon after my tea. I don't want to die of indigestion.'

'Cats have nine lives, you know,' said Sir Wilfrid heartily.

'Possibly,' answered Tobermory; 'but only one liver.'

'Adelaide!' said Mrs. Cornett, 'do you mean to encourage that cat to go out and gossip about us in the servants' hall?'

The panic had indeed become general. A narrow ornamental balustrade ran in front of most of the bedroom windows at the Towers, and it was recalled with dismay that this had formed a favourite promenade for Tobermory at all hours, whence he could watch the pigeons—and heaven knew what else besides. If he intended to become reminiscent in his present outspoken strain the effect would be something more than disconcerting. Mrs. Cornett, who spent much time at her toilet table, and whose complexion was reputed to be of a nomadic though punctual disposition, looked as ill at ease as the Major. Miss Scrawen, who wrote fiercely sensuous poetry and led a blameless life, merely displayed irritation; if you are methodical and virtuous in private you don't necessarily want every one to know it. Bertie van Tahn, who was so depraved at seventeen that he had long ago given up trying to be any worse, turned a dull shade of gardenia white, but he did not commit the error of dashing out of the room like Odo Finsberry, a young gentleman who was understood to be reading for the Church and who was possibly disturbed at the thought of scandals he might hear concerning other people. Clovis had the presence of mind to maintain a composed exterior; privately he was calculating how long it would take to procure a box of fancy mice through the agency of the *Exchange and Mart* as a species of hush-money.

Even in a delicate situation like the present, Agnes Resker could not endure to remain too long in the background.

'Why did I ever come down here?' she asked dramatically.

Tobermory immediately accepted the opening.

'Judging by what you said to Mrs. Cornett on the croquet-lawn yesterday, you were out for food. You described the Blemleys as the dullest people to stay with that you knew, but said they were clever enough to employ a first-rate cook; otherwise they'd find it difficult to get anyone to come down a second time.'

'There's not a word of truth in it! I appeal to Mrs. Cornett——' exclaimed the discomfited Agnes.

'Mrs. Cornett repeated your remark afterwards to Bertie van Tahn,' continued Tobermory, 'and said, "That woman is a regular Hunger Marcher; she'd go anywhere for four square meals a day," and Bertie van Tahn said——'

At this point the chronicle mercifully ceased. Tobermory had caught a glimpse of the big yellow Tom from the Rectory working his way through the shrubbery towards the stable wing. In a flash he had vanished through the open French window.

With the disappearance of his too brilliant pupil Cornelius Appin found himself beset by a hurricane of bitter upbraiding, anxious inquiry, and frightened entreaty. The responsibility for the situation lay with him, and he must prevent matters from becoming worse. Could Tobermory impart his dangerous gift to other cats? was the first question he had to answer. It was possible, he replied, that he might have initiated his intimate friend the stable puss into his new accomplishment, but it was unlikely that his teaching could have taken a wider range as yet.

'Then,' said Mrs. Cornett, 'Tobermory may be a valuable cat and a great pet; but I'm sure you'll agree, Adelaide, that both he and the stable cat must be done away with without delay.'

'You don't suppose I've enjoyed the last quarter of an hour, do you?' said Lady Blemley bitterly. 'My husband and I are very fond of Tobermory—at least, we were before this horrible accomplishment was infused into him; but now, of course, the only thing is to have him destroyed as soon as possible.'

' We can put some strychnine in the scraps he always gets at dinner-time,' said Sir Wilfrid, 'and I will go and drown the stable cat myself.   The coachman will be very sore at losing his pet, but I'll say a very catching form of mange has broken out in both cats and we're afraid of it spreading to the kennels.'

' But my great discovery!' expostulated Mr. Appin; ' after all my years of research and experiment——'

' You can go and experiment on the shorthorns at the farm, who are under proper control,' said Mrs. Cornett, ' or the elephants at the Zoological Gardens.   They're said to be highly intelligent, and they have this recommendation, that they don't come creeping about our bedrooms and under chairs, and so forth.'

An archangel ecstatically proclaiming the Millennium, and then finding that it clashed unpardonably with Henley and would have to be indefinitely postponed, could hardly have felt more crestfallen than Cornelius Appin at the reception of his wonderful achievement.   Public opinion, however, was against him—in fact, had the general voice been consulted on the subject it is probable that a strong minority vote would have been in favour of including him in the strychnine diet.

Defective train arrangements and a nervous desire to see matters brought to a finish prevented an immediate dispersal of the party, but dinner that evening was not a social success. Sir Wilfrid had had rather a trying time with the stable cat and subsequently with the coachman.   Agnes Resker ostentatiously limited her repast to a morsel of dry toast, which she bit as though it were a personal enemy; while Mavis Pellington maintained a vindictive silence throughout the meal.   Lady Blemley kept up a flow of what she hoped was conversation, but her attention was fixed on the doorway.   A plateful of carefully dosed fish scraps was in readiness on the sideboard, but sweets and savoury and dessert went their way, and no Tobermory appeared either in the dining-room or kitchen.

The sepulchral dinner was cheerful compared with the subsequent vigil in the smoking-room. Eating and drinking had at least supplied a distraction and cloak to the prevailing embarrassment. Bridge was out of the question in the general tension of nerves and tempers, and after Odo Finsberry had given a lugubrious rendering of ' Melisande in the Wood ' to a frigid audience, music was tacitly avoided. At eleven the servants went to bed, announcing that the small window in the pantry had been left open as usual for Tobermory's private use. The guests read steadily through the current batch of magazines, and fell back gradually on the ' Badminton Library ' and bound volumes of *Punch*. Lady Blemley made periodic visits to the pantry, returning each time with an expression of listless depression which forestalled questioning.

At two o'clock Clovis broke the dominating silence.

' He won't turn up to-night. He's probably in the local newspaper office at the present moment, dictating the first instalment of his reminiscences. Lady What's-her-name's book won't be in it. It will be the event of the day.'

Having made this contribution to the general cheerfulness, Clovis went to bed. At long intervals the various members of the house-party followed his example.

The servants taking round the early tea made a uniform announcement in reply to a uniform question. Tobermory had not returned.

Breakfast was, if anything, a more unpleasant function than dinner had been, but before its conclusion the situation was relieved. Tobermory's corpse was brought in from the shrubbery, where a gardener had just discovered it. From the bites on his throat and the yellow fur which coated his claws it was evident that he had fallen in unequal combat with the big Tom from the Rectory.

By midday most of the guests had quitted the Towers, and after lunch Lady Blemley had sufficiently recovered her spirits to write an extremely nasty letter to the Rectory about the loss of her valuable pet.

Tobermory had been Appin's one successful pupil, and he was destined to have no successor. A few weeks later an elephant in the Dresden Zoological Garden, which had shown no previous signs of irritability, broke loose and killed an Englishman who had apparently been teasing it. The victim's name was variously reported in the papers as Oppin and Eppelin, but his front name was faithfully rendered Cornelius.

' If he was trying German irregular verbs on the poor beast,' said Clovis, ' he deserved all he got.'

MRS. PACKLETIDE'S TIGER

IT was Mrs. Packletide's pleasure and intention that she should shoot a tiger. Not that the lust to kill had suddenly descended on her, or that she felt that she would leave India safer and more wholesome than she had found it, with one fraction less of wild beast per million of inhabitants. The compelling motive for her sudden deviation towards the footsteps of Nimrod was the fact that Loona Bimberton had recently been carried eleven miles in an aeroplane by an Algerian aviator, and talked of nothing else; only a personally procured tiger-skin and a heavy harvest of Press photographs could successfully counter that sort of thing. Mrs. Packletide had already arranged in her mind the lunch she would give at her house in Curzon Street, ostensibly in Loona Bimberton's honour, with a tiger-skin rug occupying most of the foreground and all of the conversation. She had also already designed in her mind the tiger-claw brooch that she was going to give Loona Bimberton on her next birthday. In a world that is supposed to be chiefly swayed by hunger and by love Mrs. Packletide was an exception; her movements and motives were largely governed by dislike of Loona Bimberton.

Circumstances proved propitious. Mrs. Packletide had offered a thousand rupees for the opportunity of shooting a tiger without overmuch risk or exertion, and it so happened that a neighbouring village could boast of being the favoured rendezvous of an animal of respectable antecedents, which had been driven by the increasing infirmities of age to abandon game-killing and confine its appetite to the smaller domestic animals. The prospect of earning the thousand rupees had stimulated the sporting and commercial instinct of the villagers; children were posted night and day on the outskirts of the local jungle to head the tiger back in the unlikely event of his attempting to roam away to fresh hunting-grounds, and the cheaper kinds of goats were left about with elaborate carelessness to keep him satisfied with his present quarters. The one great anxiety was lest he should die of old age before the date appointed for the memsahib's shoot. Mothers carrying their babies home through the jungle after the day's work in the fields hushed their singing lest they might curtail the restful sleep of the venerable herd-robber.

The great night duly arrived, moonlit and cloudless. A platform had been constructed in a comfortable and conveniently placed tree, and thereon crouched Mrs. Packletide and her paid companion, Miss Mebbin. A goat, gifted with a particularly persistent bleat, such as even a partially deaf tiger might be reasonably expected to hear on a still night, was tethered at the correct distance. With an accurately sighted rifle and a thumb-nail pack of patience cards the sportswoman awaited the coming of the quarry.

'I suppose we are in some danger?' said Miss Mebbin.

She was not actually nervous about the wild beast, but she had a morbid dread of performing an atom more service than she had been paid for.

'Nonsense,' said Mrs. Packletide; 'it's a very old tiger. It couldn't spring up here even if it wanted to.'

'If it's an old tiger I think you ought to get it cheaper. A thousand rupees is a lot of money.'

Louisa Mebbin adopted a protective elder-sister attitude towards money in general, irrespective of nationality or denomination. Her energetic intervention had saved many a rouble from dissipating itself in tips in some Moscow hotel, and francs and centimes clung to her instinctively under circumstances which would have driven them headlong from less sympathetic hands. Her speculations as to the market depreciation of tiger remnants were cut short by the appearance on the scene of the animal itself. As soon as it caught sight of the tethered goat it lay flat on the earth, seemingly less from a desire to take advantage of all available cover than for the purpose of snatching a short rest before commencing the grand attack.

' I believe it's ill,' said Louisa Mebbin, loudly in Hindustani, for the benefit of the village headman, who was in ambush in a neighbouring tree.

' Hush!' said Mrs. Packletide, and at that moment the tiger commenced ambling towards his victim.

' Now, now!' urged Miss Mebbin with some excitement; ' if he doesn't touch the goat we needn't pay for it.' (The bait was an extra.)

The rifle flashed out with a loud report, and the great tawny beast sprang to one side and then rolled over in the stillness of death. In a moment a crowd of excited natives had swarmed on to the scene, and their shouting speedily carried the glad news to the village, where a thumping of tom-toms took up the chorus of triumph. And their triumph and rejoicing found a ready echo in the heart of Mrs. Packletide; already that luncheon-party in Curzon Street seemed immeasurably nearer.

It was Louisa Mebbin who drew attention to the fact that the goat was in death-throes from a mortal bullet-wound, while no trace of the rifle's deadly work could be found on the tiger. Evidently the wrong animal had been hit, and the beast of prey had succumbed to heart-failure, caused by the sudden report of the rifle, accelerated by senile decay. Mrs. Packletide was pardonably annoyed at the discovery; but, at any rate, she was the possessor of a dead tiger, and the villagers, anxious for the thousand rupees, gladly connived at the fiction that she had shot the beast. And Miss Mebbin was a paid companion. Therefore did Mrs. Packletide face the cameras with a light heart, and her pictured fame reached from the pages of the *Texas Weekly Snapshot* to the illustrated Monday supplement of the *Novoe Vremya*. As for Loona Bimberton, she refused to look at an illustrated paper for weeks, and her letter of thanks for the gift of a tiger-claw brooch was a model of repressed emotions. The luncheon-party she declined; there are limits beyond which repressed emotions become dangerous.

From Curzon Street the tiger-skin rug travelled down to the Manor House, and was duly inspected and admired by the county, and it seemed a fitting and appropriate thing when Mrs. Packletide went to the County Costume Ball in the character of Diana. She refused to fall in, however, with Clovis's tempting suggestion of a primeval dance party, at which every one should wear the skins of beasts they had recently slain. 'I should be in rather a Baby Bunting condition,' confessed Clovis, 'with a miserable rabbit-skin or two to wrap up in, but then,' he added, with a rather malicious glance at Diana's proportions, 'my figure is quite as good as that Russian dancing boy's.'

'How amused every one would be if they knew what really happened,' said Louisa Mebbin a few days after the ball.

'What do you mean?' asked Mrs. Packletide quickly.

'How you shot the goat and frightened the tiger to death,' said Miss Mebbin, with her disagreeably pleasant laugh.

'No one would believe it,' said Mrs. Packletide, her face changing colour as rapidly as though it were going through a book of patterns before post-time.

'Loona Bimberton would,' said Miss Mebbin. Mrs. Packletide's face settled on an unbecoming shade of greenish white.

'You surely wouldn't give me away?' she asked.

'I've seen a week-end cottage near Dorking that I should rather like to buy,' said Miss Mebbin with seeming irrelevance. 'Six hundred and eighty, freehold. Quite a bargain, only I don't happen to have the money.'

.   .   .

Louisa Mebbin's pretty week-end cottage, christened by her 'Les Fauves,' and gay in summer-time with its garden borders of tiger-lilies, is the wonder and admiration of her friends.

'It is a marvel how Louisa manages to do it,' is the general verdict.

Mrs. Packletide indulges in no more big-game shooting.

'The incidental expenses are so heavy,' she confides to inquiring friends.

THE STAMPEDING OF LADY
BASTABLE

' IT would be rather nice if you would put Clovis up for another six days while I go up north to the MacGregors',' said Mrs. Sangrail sleepily across the breakfast-table. It was her invariable plan to speak in a sleepy, comfortable voice whenever she was unusually keen about anything; it put people off their guard, and they frequently fell in with her wishes before they had realized that she was really asking for anything. Lady Bastable, however, was not so easily taken unawares; possibly she knew that voice and what it betokened—at any rate, she knew Clovis.

She frowned at a piece of toast and ate it very slowly, as though she wished to convey the impression that the process hurt her more than it hurt the toast; but no extension of hospitality on Clovis's behalf rose to her lips.

' It would be a great convenience to me,' pursued Mrs. Sangrail, abandoning the careless tone. ' I particularly don't want to take him to the MacGregors', and it will only be for six days.'

' It will seem longer,' said Lady Bastable dismally. ' The last time he stayed here for a week——'

' I know,' interrupted the other hastily, ' but that was nearly two years ago. He was younger then.'

' But he hasn't improved,' said her hostess; ' it's no use growing older if you only learn new ways of misbehaving yourself.'

Mrs. Sangrail was unable to argue the point; since Clovis had reached the age of seventeen she had never ceased to bewail his irrepressible waywardness to all her circle of acquaintances, and a polite scepticism would have greeted the slightest hint at a prospective reformation. She discarded the fruitless effort at cajolery and resorted to undisguised bribery.

'If you'll have him here for these six days I'll cancel that outstanding bridge account.'

It was only for forty-nine shillings, but Lady Bastable loved shillings with a great, strong love. To lose money at bridge and not to have to pay it was one of those rare experiences which gave the card-table a glamour in her eyes which it could never otherwise have possessed. Mrs. Sangrail was almost equally devoted to her card winnings, but the prospect of conveniently warehousing her offspring for six days, and incidentally saving his railway fare to the north, reconciled her to the sacrifice; when Clovis made a belated appearance at the breakfast-table the bargain had been struck.

'Just think,' said Mrs. Sangrail sleepily; 'Lady Bastable has very kindly asked you to stay on here while I go to the Mac-Gregors'.'

Clovis said suitable things in a highly unsuitable manner, and proceeded to make punitive expeditions among the breakfast dishes with a scowl on his face that would have driven the purr out of a peace conference. The arrangement that had been concluded behind his back was doubly distasteful to him. In the first place, he particularly wanted to teach the MacGregor boys, who could well afford the knowledge, how to play poker-patience; secondly, the Bastable catering was of the kind that is classified as a rude plenty, which Clovis translated as a plenty that gives rise to rude remarks. Watching him from behind ostentatiously sleepy lids, his mother realized, in the light of long experience, that any rejoicing over the success of her manœuvre would be distinctly premature. It was one thing to fit Clovis into a convenient niche of the domestic jig-saw puzzle; it was quite another matter to get him to stay there.

Lady Bastable was wont to retire in state to the morning-room immediately after breakfast and spend a quiet hour in skimming through the papers; they were there, so she might as well get their money's worth out of them. Politics did not greatly interest her, but she was obsessed with a favourite foreboding that one of these days there would be a great social upheaval, in which everybody would be killed by everybody else. 'It will come sooner than we think,' she would observe darkly; a mathematical expert of exceptionally high powers would have been puzzled to work out the approximate date from the slender and confusing groundwork which this assertion afforded.

On this particular morning the sight of Lady Bastable enthroned among her papers gave Clovis the hint towards which his mind had been groping all breakfast time. His mother had gone upstairs to supervise packing operations, and he was alone on the ground-floor with his hostess—and the servants. The latter were the key to the situation. Bursting wildly into the kitchen quarters, Clovis screamed a frantic though strictly non-committal summons: 'Poor Lady Bastable! In the morning-room! Oh, quick!' The next moment the butler, cook, page-boy, two or three maids, and a gardener who had happened to be in one of the outer kitchens were following in a hot scurry after Clovis as he headed back for the morning-room. Lady Bastable was roused from the world of newspaper lore by hearing a Japanese screen in the hall go down with a crash. Then the door leading from the hall flew open and her young guest tore madly through the room, shrieked at her in passing, 'The jacquerie! They're on us!' and dashed like an escaping hawk out through the French window. The scared mob of servants burst in on his heels, the gardener still clutching the sickle with which he had been trimming hedges, and the impetus of their headlong haste carried them, slipping and sliding, over the smooth parquet flooring towards the chair where their mistress sat in panic-stricken amazement. If she had had a moment granted her for reflection she would have behaved, as she afterwards explained, with considerable dignity. It was probably the sickle which decided her, but anyway she followed the lead that Clovis had given her through the French window, and ran well and far across the lawn before the eyes of her astonished retainers.

·   ·   ·

Lost dignity is not a possession which can be restored at a moment's notice, and both Lady Bastable and the butler found the process of returning to normal conditions almost as painful as a slow recovery from drowning.   A jacquerie, even if carried out with the most respectful of intentions, cannot fail to leave some traces of embarrassment behind it.   By lunch-time, however, decorum had reasserted itself with enhanced rigour as a natural rebound from its recent overthrow, and the meal was served in a frigid stateliness that might have been framed on a Byzantine model.   Half-way through its duration Mrs. Sangrail was solemnly presented with an envelope lying on a silver salver.   It contained a cheque for forty-nine shillings.

The MacGregor boys learned how to play poker-patience; after all, they could afford to.

THE BACKGROUND

' THAT woman's art-jargon tires me,' said Clovis to his journalist friend. ' She's so fond of talking of certain pictures as " growing on one," as though they were a sort of fungus.'

' That reminds me,' said the journalist, ' of the story of Henri Deplis. Have I ever told it you?'

Clovis shook his head.

' Henri Deplis was by birth a native of the Grand Duchy of Luxemburg. On maturer reflection he became a commercial traveller. His business activities frequently took him beyond the limits of the Grand Duchy, and he was stopping in a small town of Northern Italy when news reached him from home that a legacy from a distant and deceased relative had fallen to his share.

' It was not a large legacy, even from the modest standpoint of Henri Deplis, but it impelled him towards some seemingly harmless extravagances. In particular it led him to patronize local art as represented by the tattoo-needles of Signor Andreas Pincini. Signor Pincini was, perhaps, the most brilliant master of tattoo craft that Italy had ever known, but his circumstances were decidedly impoverished, and for the sum of six hundred francs he gladly undertook to cover his client's back, from the collar-bone down to the waist-line, with a glowing representation of the Fall of Icarus. The design, when finally developed, was a slight disappointment to Monsieur Deplis, who had suspected Icarus of being a fortress taken by Wallenstein in the Thirty Years' War, but he was more than satisfied with the execution of the work, which was acclaimed by all who had the privilege of seeing it as Pincini's masterpiece.

' It was his greatest effort, and his last. Without even waiting to be paid, the illustrious craftsman departed this life, and was buried under an ornate tombstone, whose winged cherubs would have afforded singularly little scope for the exercise of his favourite art. There remained, however, the widow Pincini, to whom the six hundred francs were due. And thereupon arose the great crisis in the life of Henri Deplis, traveller of commerce. The legacy, under the stress of numerous little calls on its substance, had dwindled to very insignificant proportions, and when a pressing wine bill and sundry other current accounts had been paid, there remained little more than 430 francs to offer to the widow. The lady was properly indignant, not wholly, as she volubly explained, on account of the suggested writing-off of 170 francs, but also at the attempt to depreciate the value of her late husband's acknowledged masterpiece. In a week's time Deplis was obliged to reduce his offer to 405 francs, which circumstance fanned the widow's indignation into a fury. She cancelled the sale of the work of art, and a few days later Deplis learned with a sense of consternation that she had presented it to the municipality of Bergamo, which had gratefully accepted it. He left the neighbourhood as unobtrusively as possible, and was genuinely relieved when his business commands took him to Rome, where he hoped his identity and that of the famous picture might be lost sight of.

' But he bore on his back the burden of the dead man's genius. On presenting himself one day in the steaming corridor of a vapour bath, he was at once hustled back into his clothes by the proprietor, who was a North Italian, and who emphatically refused to allow the celebrated Fall of Icarus to be publicly on view without the permission of the municipality of Bergamo. Public interest and official vigilance increased as the matter became more widely known, and Deplis was unable to take a simple dip in the sea or river on the hottest afternoon unless clothed up to the collar-bone in a substantial bathing garment. Later on the authorities of Bergamo conceived the idea that salt water might be injurious to the masterpiece, and a perpetual injunction was obtained which debarred the muchly harassed commercial traveller from sea bathing under any circumstances. Altogether, he was fervently thankful when his firm of employers found him a new range of activities in the neighbourhood of

Bordeaux. His thankfulness, however, ceased abruptly at the Franco-Italian frontier. An imposing array of official force barred his departure, and he was sternly reminded of the stringent law which forbids the exportation of Italian works of art.

'A diplomatic parley ensued between the Luxemburgian and Italian Governments, and at one time the European situation became overcast with the possibilities of trouble. But the Italian Government stood firm; it declined to concern itself in the least with the fortunes or even the existence of Henri Deplis, commercial traveller, but was immovable in its decision that the Fall of Icarus (by the late Pincini, Andreas) at present the property of the municipality of Bergamo, should not leave the country.

'The excitement died down in time, but the unfortunate Deplis, who was of a constitutionally retiring disposition, found himself a few months later once more the storm-centre of a furious controversy. A certain German art expert, who had obtained from the municipality of Bergamo permission to inspect the famous masterpiece, declared it to be a spurious Pincini, probably the work of some pupil whom he had employed in his declining years. The evidence of Deplis on the subject was obviously worthless, as he had been under the influence of the customary narcotics during the long process of pricking in the design. The editor of an Italian art journal refuted the contentions of the German expert and undertook to prove that his private life did not conform to any modern standard of decency. The whole of Italy and Germany were drawn into the dispute, and the rest of Europe was soon involved in the quarrel. There were stormy scenes in the Spanish Parliament, and the University of Copenhagen bestowed a gold medal on the German expert (afterwards sending a commission to examine his proofs on the spot), while two Polish schoolboys in Paris committed suicide to show what *they* thought of the matter.

'Meanwhile, the unhappy human background fared no better

than before, and it was not surprising that he drifted into the ranks of Italian anarchists.   Four times at least he was escorted to the frontier as a dangerous and undesirable foreigner, but he was always brought back as the Fall of Icarus (attributed to Pincini, Andreas, early Twentieth Century).   And then one day, at an anarchist congress at Genoa, a fellow-worker, in the heat of debate, broke a phial full of corrosive liquid over his back.   The red shirt that he was wearing mitigated the effects, but the Icarus was ruined beyond recognition.   His assailant was severely reprimanded for assaulting a fellow-anarchist and received seven years' imprisonment for defacing a national art treasure   As soon as he was able to leave the hospital Henri Deplis was put across the frontier as an undesirable alien.

' In the quieter streets of Paris, especially in the neighbour-hood of the Ministry of Fine Arts, you may sometimes meet a depressed, anxious-looking man, who, if you pass him the time of day, will answer you with a slight Luxemburgian accent. He nurses the illusion that he is one of the lost arms of the Venus de Milo, and hopes that the French Government may be persuaded to buy him.   On all other subjects I believe he is tolerably sane.'

HERMANN THE IRASCIBLE
A STORY OF THE GREAT WEEP

IT was in the second decade of the twentieth century, after the Great Plague had devastated England, that Hermann the Irascible, nicknamed also the Wise, sat on the British throne. The Mortal Sickness had swept away the entire Royal Family, unto the third and fourth generations, and thus it came to pass that Hermann the Fourteenth of Saxe-Drachsen-Wachtelstein, who had stood thirtieth in the order of succession, found himself one day ruler of the British dominions within and beyond the seas. He was one of the unexpected things that happen in politics, and he happened with great thoroughness. In many ways he was the most progressive monarch who had sat on an important throne; before people knew where they were, they were somewhere else. Even his Ministers, progressive though they were by tradition, found it difficult to keep pace with his legislative suggestions.

'As a matter of fact,' admitted the Prime Minister, 'we are hampered by these votes-for-women creatures; they disturb our meetings throughout the country, and they try to turn Downing Street into a sort of political picnic-ground.'

'They must be dealt with,' said Hermann.

'Dealt with,' said the Prime Minister; 'exactly, just so; but how?'

'I will draft you a Bill,' said the King, sitting down at his typewriting machine, 'enacting that women shall vote at all future elections. *Shall* vote, you observe; or, to put it plainer, must. Voting will remain optional, as before, for male electors; but every woman between the ages of twenty-one and seventy will be obliged to vote, not only at elections for Parliament, county councils, district boards, parish councils, and municipalities, but for coroners, school inspectors, churchwardens, curators of museums, sanitary authorities, police-court interpreters, swimming-bath instructors, contractors, choir-masters, market superintendents, art-school teachers, cathedral vergers, and other local functionaries whose names I will add as they occur to me. All these offices will become elective, and failure to vote at any election falling within her area of residence will involve the female elector in a penalty of £10. Absence, unsupported by an adequate medical certificate, will not be accepted as an excuse. Pass this Bill through the two Houses of Parliament, and bring it to me for signature the day after to-morrow.'

From the very outset the Compulsory Female Franchise produced little or no elation even in circles which had been loudest in demanding the vote. The bulk of the women of the country had been indifferent or hostile to the franchise agitation, and the most fanatical Suffragettes began to wonder what they had found so attractive in the prospect of putting ballot-papers into a box. In the country districts the task of carrying out the provisions of the new Act was irksome enough; in the towns and cities it became an incubus. There seemed no end to the elections. Laundresses and seamstresses had to hurry away from their work to vote, often for a candidate whose name they hadn't heard before, and whom they selected at haphazard; female clerks and waitresses got up extra early to get their voting done before starting off to their places of business. Society women found their arrangements impeded and upset by the continual necessity for attending the polling stations, and week-end parties and summer holidays became gradually a masculine luxury. As for Cairo and the Riviera, they were possible only for genuine invalids or people of enormous wealth, for the accumulation of £10 fines during a prolonged absence was a contingency that even ordinarily wealthy folk could hardly afford to risk.

It was not wonderful that the female disfranchisement agitation became a formidable movement. The No-Votes-for-Women League numbered its feminine adherents by the million; its colours, citron and old Dutch-madder, were flaunted everywhere, and its battle hymn, ' We don't want to Vote,' became a popular refrain.   As the Government showed no signs of being impressed by peaceful persuasion, more violent methods came into vogue.   Meetings were disturbed, Ministers were mobbed, policemen were bitten, and ordinary prison fare rejected, and on the eve of the anniversary of Trafalgar women bound themselves in tiers up the entire length of the Nelson column so that its customary floral decoration had to be abandoned.   Still the Government obstinately adhered to its conviction that women ought to have the vote.

Then, as a last resort, some woman wit hit upon an expedient which it was strange that no one had thought of before.   The Great Weep was organized.   Relays of women, ten thousand at a time, wept continuously in the public places of the Metropolis.   They wept in railway stations, in tubes and omnibuses, in the National Gallery, at the Army and Navy Stores, in St. James's Park, at ballad concerts, at Prince's and in the Burlington Arcade.   The hitherto unbroken success of the brilliant farcical comedy ' Henry's Rabbit ' was imperilled by the presence of drearily weeping women in stalls and circle and gallery, and one of the brightest divorce cases that had been tried for many years was robbed of much of its sparkle by the lachrymose behaviour of a section of the audience.

' What are we to do? ' asked the Prime Minister, whose cook had wept into all the breakfast dishes and whose nursemaid had gone out, crying quietly and miserably, to take the children for a walk in the Park.

' There is a time for everything,' said the King; ' there is a time to yield.   Pass a measure through the two Houses depriving women of the right to vote, and bring it to me for the Royal assent the day after to-morrow."

As the Minister withdrew, Hermann the Irascible, who was also nicknamed the Wise, gave a profound chuckle.

' There are more ways of killing a cat than by choking it with cream,' he quoted, 'but I'm not sure,' he added, ' that it's not the best way.'

THE UNREST-CURE

ON the rack in the railway carriage immediately opposite Clovis was a solidly wrought travelling-bag, with a carefully written label, on which was inscribed, ' J. P. Huddle, The Warren, Tilfield, near Slowborough.' Immediately below the rack sat the human embodiment of the label, a solid, sedate individual, sedately dressed, sedately conversational. Even without his conversation (which was addressed to a friend seated by his side, and touched chiefly on such topics as the backwardness of Roman hyacinths and the prevalence of measles at the Rectory), one could have gauged fairly accurately the temperament and mental outlook of the travelling bag's owner. But he seemed unwilling to leave anything to the imagination of a casual observer, and his talk grew presently personal and introspective.

' I don't know how it is,' he told his friend, ' I'm not much over forty, but I seem to have settled down into a deep groove of elderly middle-age. My sister shows the same tendency. We like everything to be exactly in its accustomed place; we like things to happen exactly at their appointed times; we like everything to be usual, orderly, punctual, methodical, to a hair's breadth, to a minute. It distresses and upsets us if it is not so. For instance, to take a very trifling matter, a thrush has built its nest year after year in the catkin-tree on the lawn; this year, for no obvious reason, it is building in the ivy on the garden wall. We have said very little about it, but I think we both feel that the change is unnecessary, and just a little irritating.'

' Perhaps,' said the friend, ' it is a different thrush.'

' We have suspected that,' said J. P. Huddle, ' and I think it gives us even more cause for annoyance. We don't feel that we want a change of thrush at our time of life; and yet, as I have said, we have scarcely reached an age when these things should make themselves seriously felt.'

' What you want,' said the friend, ' is an Unrest-cure.'

' An Unrest-cure? I've never heard of such a thing.'

' You've heard of Rest-cures for people who've broken down under stress of too much worry and strenuous living; well, you're suffering from overmuch repose and placidity, and you need the opposite kind of treatment.'

' But where would one go for such a thing? '

' Well, you might stand as an Orange candidate for Kilkenny, or do a course of district visiting in one of the Apache quarters of Paris, or give lectures in Berlin to prove that most of Wagner's music was written by Gambetta; and there's always the interior of Morocco to travel in. But, to be really effective, the Unrest-cure ought to be tried in the home. How you would do it I haven't the faintest idea.'

It was at this point in the conversation that Clovis became galvanized into alert attention. After all, his two days' visit to an elderly relative at Slowborough did not promise much excitement. Before the train had stopped he had decorated his sinister shirt-cuff with the inscription, ' J. P. Huddle, The Warren, Tilfield, near Slowborough.'

.   .   .

Two mornings later Mr. Huddle broke in on his sister's privacy as she sat reading *Country Life* in the morning room. It was her day and hour and place for reading *Country Life*, and the intrusion was absolutely irregular; but he bore in his hand a telegram, and in that household telegrams were recognized as happening by the hand of God. This particular telegram partook of the nature of a thunderbolt. ' Bishop examining confirmation class in neighbourhood unable stay rectory on account measles invokes your hospitality sending secretary arrange.'

' I scarcely know the Bishop; I've only spoken to him once,' exclaimed J. P. Huddle, with the exculpating air of one who realizes too late the indiscretion of speaking to strange Bishops. Miss Huddle was the first to rally; she disliked thunderbolts as fervently as her brother did, but the womanly instinct in her told her that thunderbolts must be fed.

'We can curry the cold duck,' she said. It was not the appointed day for curry, but the little orange envelope involved a certain departure from rule and custom. Her brother said nothing, but his eyes thanked her for being brave.

'A young gentleman to see you,' announced the parlour-maid.

'The secretary!' murmured the Huddles in unison; they instantly stiffened into a demeanour which proclaimed that, though they held all strangers to be guilty, they were willing to hear anything they might have to say in their defence. The young gentleman, who came into the room with a certain elegant haughtiness, was not at all Huddle's idea of a bishop's secretary; he had not supposed that the episcopal establishment could have afforded such an expensively upholstered article when there were so many other claims on its resources. The face was fleetingly familiar; if he had bestowed more attention on the fellow-traveller sitting opposite him in the railway carriage two days before he might have recognized Clovis in his present visitor.

'You are the Bishop's secretary?' asked Huddle, becoming consciously deferential.

'His confidential secretary,' answered Clovis. 'You may call me Stanislaus; my other name doesn't matter. The Bishop and Colonel Alberti may be here to lunch. I shall be here in any case.'

It sounded rather like the programme of a Royal visit.

'The Bishop is examining a confirmation class in the neighbourhood, isn't he?' asked Miss Huddle.

'Ostensibly,' was the dark reply, followed by a request for a large-scale map of the locality.

Clovis was still immersed in a seemingly profound study of the map when another telegram arrived. It was addressed to 'Prince Stanislaus, care of Huddle, The Warren, etc.' Clovis glanced at the contents and announced: 'The Bishop and Alberti won't be here till late in the afternoon.' Then he returned to his scrutiny of the map.

The luncheon was not a very festive function. The princely secretary ate and drank with fair appetite, but severely discouraged conversation. At the finish of the meal he broke suddenly into a radiant smile, thanked his hostess for a charming repast, and kissed her hand with deferential rapture. Miss Huddle was unable to decide in her mind whether the action savoured of Louis Quatorzian courtliness or the reprehensible Roman attitude towards the Sabine women. It was not her day for having a headache, but she felt that the circumstances excused her, and retired to her room to have as much headache as was possible before the Bishop's arrival. Clovis, having asked the way to the nearest telegraph office, disappeared presently down the carriage drive. Mr. Huddle met him in the hall some two hours later, and asked when the Bishop would arrive.

' He is in the library with Alberti,' was the reply.

' But why wasn't I told? I never knew he had come! ' exclaimed Huddle.

' No one knows he is here,' said Clovis; ' the quieter we can keep matters the better. And on no account disturb him in the library. Those are his orders.'

' But what is all this mystery about? And who is Alberti? And isn't the Bishop going to have tea? '

' The Bishop is out for blood, not tea.'

' Blood! ' gasped Huddle, who did not find that the thunderbolt improved on acquaintance.

' To-night is going to be a great night in the history of Christendom,' said Clovis. ' We are going to massacre every Jew in the neighbourhood.'

' To massacre the Jews! ' said Huddle indignantly. ' Do you mean to tell me there's a general rising against them? '

' No, it's the Bishop's own idea. He's in there arranging all the details now.'

' But—the Bishop is such a tolerant, humane man.'

' That is precisely what will heighten the effect of his action. The sensation will be enormous.'

That at least Huddle could believe.

'He will be hanged!' he exclaimed with conviction.

'A motor is waiting to carry him to the coast, where a steam yacht is in readiness.'

'But there aren't thirty Jews in the whole neighbourhood,' protested Huddle, whose brain, under the repeated shocks of the day, was operating with the uncertainty of a telegraph wire during earthquake disturbances.

'We have twenty-six on our list,' said Clovis, referring to a bundle of notes. 'We shall be able to deal with them all the more thoroughly.'

'Do you mean to tell me that you are meditating violence against a man like Sir Leon Birberry,' stammered Huddle; 'he's one of the most respected men in the country.'

'He's down on our list,' said Clovis carelessly; 'after all, we've got men we can trust to do our job, so we shan't have to rely on local assistance. And we've got some Boy-scouts helping us as auxiliaries.'

'Boy-scouts!'

'Yes; when they understood there was real killing to be done they were even keener than the men.'

'This thing will be a blot on the Twentieth Century!'

'And your house will be the blotting-pad. Have you realized that half the papers of Europe and the United States will publish pictures of it? By the way, I've sent some photographs of you and your sister, that I found in the library, to the *Matin* and *Die Woche*; I hope you don't mind. Also a sketch of the staircase; most of the killing will probably be done on the staircase.'

The emotions that were surging in J. P. Huddle's brain were almost too intense to be disclosed in speech, but he managed to gasp out: 'There aren't any Jews in this house.'

'Not at present,' said Clovis.

'I shall go to the police,' shouted Huddle with sudden energy.

'In the shrubbery,' said Clovis, 'are posted ten men, who have orders to fire on anyone who leaves the house without my signal of permission. Another armed picquet is in ambush near the front gate. The Boy-scouts watch the back premises.'

At this moment the cheerful hoot of a motor-horn was heard from the drive. Huddle rushed to the hall door with the feeling of a man half-awakened from a nightmare, and beheld Sir Leon Birberry, who had driven himself over in his car. ' I got your telegram,' he said; ' what's up?'

Telegram? It seemed to be a day of telegrams.

' Come here at once. Urgent. James Huddle,' was the purport of the message displayed before Huddle's bewildered eyes.

' I see it all!' he exclaimed suddenly in a voice shaken with agitation, and with a look of agony in the direction of the shrubbery he hauled the astonished Birberry into the house. Tea had just been laid in the hall, but the now thoroughly panic-stricken Huddle dragged his protesting guest upstairs, and in a few minutes' time the entire household had been summoned to that region of momentary safety. Clovis alone graced the tea-table with his presence; the fanatics in the library were evidently too immersed in their monstrous machinations to dally with the solace of teacup and hot toast. Once the youth rose, in answer to the summons of the front-door bell, and admitted Mr. Paul Isaacs, shoemaker and parish councillor, who had also received a pressing invitation to The Warren. With an atrocious assumption of courtesy, which a Borgia could hardly have outdone, the secretary escorted this new captive of his net to the head of the stairway, where his involuntary host awaited him.

And then ensued a long ghastly vigil of watching and waiting. Once or twice Clovis left the house to stroll across to the shrubbery, returning always to the library, for the purpose evidently of making a brief report. Once he took in the letters from the evening postman, and brought them to the top of the stairs with punctilious politeness. After his next absence he came half-way up the stairs to make an announcement.

' The Boy-scouts mistook my signal, and have killed the

postman. I've had very little practice in this sort of thing, you see. Another time I shall do better.'

The housemaid, who was engaged to be married to the evening postman, gave way to clamorous grief.

'Remember that your mistress has a headache,' said J. P. Huddle. (Miss Huddle's headache was worse.)

Clovis hastened downstairs, and after a short visit to the library returned with another message:

'The Bishop is sorry to hear that Miss Huddle has a headache. He is issuing orders that as far as possible no firearms shall be used near the house; any killing that is necessary on the premises will be done with cold steel. The Bishop does not see why a man should not be a gentleman as well as a Christian.'

That was the last they saw of Clovis; it was nearly seven o'clock, and his elderly relative liked him to dress for dinner. But, though he had left them for ever, the lurking suggestion of his presence haunted the lower regions of the house during the long hours of the wakeful night, and every creak of the stairway, every rustle of wind through the shrubbery, was fraught with horrible meaning. At about seven next morning the gardener's boy and the early postman finally convinced the watchers that the Twentieth Century was still unblotted.

'I don't suppose,' mused Clovis, as an early train bore him townwards, 'that they will be in the least grateful for the Unrest-cure.'

THE JESTING OF
ARLINGTON STRINGHAM

ARLINGTON STRINGHAM made a joke in the House of Commons. It was a thin House, and a very thin joke; something about the Anglo-Saxon race having a great many angles. It is possible that it was unintentional, but a fellow-member, who did not wish it to be supposed that he was asleep because his eyes were shut, laughed. One or two of the papers noted 'a laugh' in brackets, and another, which was notorious for the carelessness of its political news, mentioned 'laughter.' Things often begin in that way.

'Arlington made a joke in the House last night,' said Eleanor Stringham to her mother; 'in all the years we've been married neither of us has made jokes, and I don't like it now. I'm afraid it's the beginning of the rift in the lute.'

'What lute?' said her mother.

'It's a quotation,' said Eleanor.

To say that anything was a quotation was an excellent method, in Eleanor's eyes, for withdrawing it from discussion, just as you could always defend indifferent lamb late in the season by saying 'It's mutton.'

And, of course, Arlington Stringham continued to tread the thorny path of conscious humour into which Fate had beckoned him.

'The country's looking very green, but, after all, that's what it's there for," he remarked to his wife two days later.

'That's very modern, and I dare say very clever, but I'm afraid it's wasted on me,' she observed coldly. If she had known how much effort it had cost him to make the remark she might have greeted it in a kinder spirit. It is the tragedy of human endeavour that it works so often unseen and unguessed.

Arlington said nothing, not from injured pride, but because he was thinking hard for something to say. Eleanor mistook his silence for an assumption of tolerant superiority, and her anger prompted her to a further gibe.

'You had better tell it to Lady Isobel. I've no doubt she would appreciate it.'

Lady Isobel was seen everywhere with a fawn coloured collie at a time when every one else kept nothing but Pekinese, and she had once eaten four green apples at an afternoon tea in the Botanical Gardens, so she was widely credited with a rather unpleasant wit. The censorious said she slept in a hammock and understood Yeats's poems, but her family denied both stories.

'The rift is widening to an abyss,' said Eleanor to her mother that afternoon.

'I should not tell that to anyone,' remarked her mother, after long reflection.

'Naturally, I should not talk about it very much,' said Eleanor, 'but why shouldn't I mention it to anyone?'

'Because you can't have an abyss in a lute. There isn't room."

Eleanor's outlook on life did not improve as the afternoon wore on. The page-boy had brought from the library *By Mere and Wold* instead of *By Mere Chance*, the book which every one denied having read. The unwelcome substitute appeared to be a collection of nature notes contributed by the author to the pages of some Northern weekly, and when one had been prepared to plunge with disapproving mind into a regrettable chronicle of ill-spent lives it was intensely irritating to read 'the dainty yellow-hammers are now with us, and flaunt their jaundiced livery from every bush and hillock.' Besides, the thing was so obviously untrue; either there must be hardly any bushes or hillocks in those parts or the country must be fearfully overstocked with yellow-hammers. The thing scarcely seemed worth telling such a lie about. And the page-boy stood there, with his sleekly brushed and parted hair, and his air of chaste and callous indifference to the desires and passions of the world. Eleanor hated boys, and she would have liked to have whipped this one long and often. It was perhaps the yearning of a woman who had no children of her own.

She turned at random to another paragraph. ' Lie quietly concealed in the fern and bramble in the gap by the old rowan tree, and you may see, almost every evening during early summer, a pair of lesser whitethroats creeping up and down the nettles and hedge-growth that mask their nesting-place.'

The insufferable monotony of the proposed recreation! Eleanor would not have watched the most brilliant performance at His Majesty's Theatre for a single evening under such uncomfortable circumstances, and to be asked to watch lesser whitethroats creeping up and down a nettle ' almost every evening ' during the height of the season struck her as an imputation on her intelligence that was positively offensive. Impatiently she transferred her attention to the dinner menu, which the boy had thoughtfully brought in as an alternative to the more solid literary fare. ' Rabbit curry,' met her eye, and the lines of disapproval deepened on her already puckered brow. The cook was a great believer in the influence of environment, and nourished an obstinate conviction that if you brought rabbit and curry-powder together in one dish a rabbit curry would be the result. And Clovis and the odious Bertie van Tahn were coming to dinner. Surely, thought Eleanor, if Arlington knew how much she had had that day to try her, he would refrain from joke-making.

At dinner that night it was Eleanor herself who mentioned the name of a certain statesman, who may be decently covered under the disguise of X.

' X.,' said Arlington Stringham, ' has the soul of a meringue.'

It was a useful remark to have on hand, because it applied equally well to four prominent statesmen of the day, which quadrupled the opportunities for using it.

' Meringues haven't got souls,' said Eleanor's mother.

' It's a mercy that they haven't,' said Clovis; 'they would be always losing them, and people like my aunt would get up missions to meringues, and say it was wonderful how much one could teach them and how much more one could learn from them.'

'What could you learn from a meringue?' asked Eleanor's mother.

'My aunt has been known to learn humility from an ex-Viceroy,' said Clovis.

'I wish cook would learn to make curry, or have the sense to leave it alone,' said Arlington, suddenly and savagely.

Eleanor's face softened. It was like one of his old remarks in the days when there was no abyss between them.

It was during the debate on the Foreign Office vote that Stringham made his great remark that 'the people of Crete unfortunately make more history than they can consume locally.' It was not brilliant, but it came in the middle of a dull speech, and the House was quite pleased with it. Old gentlemen with bad memories said it reminded them of Disraeli.

It was Eleanor's friend, Gertrude Ilpton, who drew her attention to Arlington's newest outbreak. Eleanor in these days avoided the morning papers.

'It's very modern, and I suppose very clever,' she observed.

'Of course it's clever,' said Gertrude; 'all Lady Isobel's sayings are clever, and luckily they bear repeating.'

'Are you sure it's one of her sayings?' asked Eleanor.

'My dear, I've heard her say it dozens of times.'

'So that is where he gets his humour,' said Eleanor slowly, and the hard lines deepened round her mouth.

The death of Eleanor Stringham from an overdose of chloral, occurring at the end of a rather uneventful season, excited a certain amount of unobtrusive speculation. Clovis, who perhaps exaggerated the importance of curry in the home, hinted at domestic sorrow.

And of course Arlington never knew. It was the tragedy of his life that he should miss the fullest effect of his jesting.

SREDNI VASHTAR

CONRADIN was ten years old, and the doctor had pronounced his professional opinion that the boy would not live another five years. The doctor was silky and effete, and counted for little, but his opinion was endorsed by Mrs. de Ropp, who counted for nearly everything. Mrs. De Ropp was Conradin's cousin and guardian, and in his eyes she represented those three-fifths of the world that are necessary and disagreeable and real; the other two-fifths, in perpetual antagonism to the foregoing, were summed up in himself and his imagination. One of these days Conradin supposed he would succumb to the mastering pressure of wearisome necessary things—such as illnesses and coddling restrictions and drawn-out dullness. Without his imagination, which was rampant under the spur of loneliness, he would have succumbed long ago.

Mrs. de Ropp would never, in her honestest moments, have confessed to herself that she disliked Conradin, though she might have been dimly aware that thwarting him ' for his good ' was a duty which she did not find particularly irksome. Conradin hated her with a desperate sincerity which he was perfectly able to mask. Such few pleasures as he could contrive for himself gained an added relish from the likelihood that they would be displeasing to his guardian, and from the realm of his imagination she was locked out—an unclean thing, which should find no entrance.

In the dull, cheerless garden, overlooked by so many windows that were ready to open with a message not to do this or that, or a reminder that medicines were due, he found little attraction. The few fruit-trees that it contained were set jealously apart from his plucking, as though they were rare specimens of their kind blooming in an arid waste; it would probably have been difficult to find a market-gardener who would have offered ten shillings for their entire yearly produce

In a forgotten corner, however, almost hidden behind a dismal shrubbery, was a disused tool-shed of respectable proportions, and within its walls Conradin found a haven, something that took on the varying aspects of a playroom and a cathedral. He had peopled it with a legion of familiar phantoms, evoked partly from fragments of history and partly from his own brain, but it also boasted two inmates of flesh and blood. In one corner lived a ragged-plumaged Houdan hen, on which the boy lavished an affection that had scarcely another outlet. Further back in the gloom stood a large hutch, divided into two compartments, one of which was fronted with close iron bars. This was the abode of a large polecat-ferret, which a friendly butcher-boy had once smuggled, cage and all, into its present quarters, in exchange for a long-secreted hoard of small silver. Conradin was dreadfully afraid of the lithe, sharp-fanged beast, but it was his most treasured possession. Its very presence in the tool-shed was a secret and fearful joy, to be kept scrupulously from the knowledge of the Woman, as he privately dubbed his cousin. And one day, out of Heaven knows what material, he spun the beast a wonderful name, and from that moment it grew into a god and a religion. The Woman indulged in religion once a week at a church near by, and took Conradin with her, but to him the church service was an alien rite in the House of Rimmon. Every Thursday, in the dim and musty silence of the tool-shed, he worshipped with mystic and elaborate ceremonial before the wooden hutch where dwelt Sredni Vashtar, the great ferret. Red flowers in their season and scarlet berries in the winter-time were offered at his shrine, for he was a god who laid some special stress on the fierce impatient side of things, as opposed to the Woman's religion, which, as far as Conradin could observe, went to great lengths in the contrary direction. And on great festivals powdered nutmeg was strewn in front of his hutch, an important feature of the offering being that the nutmeg had to be stolen. These festivals were of irregular occurrence, and were chiefly appointed to celebrate some passing event. On one occasion, when Mrs.

de Ropp suffered from acute toothache for three days, Conradin kept up the festival during the entire three days, and almost succeeded in persuading himself that Sredni Vashtar was personally responsible for the toothache. If the malady had lasted for another day the supply of nutmeg would have given out.

The Houdan hen was never drawn into the cult of Sredni Vashtar. Conradin had long ago settled that she was an Anabaptist. He did not pretend to have the remotest knowledge as to what an Anabaptist was, but he privately hoped that it was dashing and not very respectable. Mrs. de Ropp was the ground plan on which he based and detested all respectability.

After a while Conradin's absorption in the tool-shed began to attract the notice of his guardian. ' It is not good for him to be pottering down there in all weathers,' she promptly decided, and at breakfast one morning she announced that the Houdan hen had been sold and taken away overnight. With her short-sighted eyes she peered at Conradin, waiting for an outbreak of rage and sorrow, which she was ready to rebuke with a flow of excellent precepts and reasoning. But Conradin said nothing: there was nothing to be said. Something perhaps in his white set face gave her a momentary qualm, for at tea that afternoon there was toast on the table, a delicacy which she usually banned on the ground that it was bad for him; also because the making of it ' gave trouble,' a deadly offence in the middle-class feminine eye.

' I thought you liked toast,' she exclaimed, with an injured air, observing that he did not touch it.

' Sometimes,' said Conradin.

In the shed that evening there was an innovation in the worship of the hutch-god. Conradin had been wont to chant his praises, to-night he asked a boon.

' Do one thing for me, Sredni Vashtar.'

The thing was not specified. As Sredni Vashtar was a god he must be supposed to know. And choking back a sob as he looked at that other empty corner, Conradin went back to the world he so hated.

And every night, in the welcome darkness of his bedroom, and every evening in the dusk of the tool-shed, Conradin's bitter litany went up: ' Do one thing for me, Sredni Vashtar.'

Mrs. de Ropp noticed that the visits to the shed did not cease, and one day she made a further journey of inspection.

' What are you keeping in that locked hutch?' she asked. ' I believe it's guinea-pigs. I'll have them all cleared away.'

Conradin shut his lips tight, but the Woman ransacked his bedroom till she found the carefully hidden key, and forthwith marched down to the shed to complete her discovery. It was a cold afternoon, and Conradin had been bidden to keep to the house. From the furthest window of the dining-room the door of the shed could just be seen beyond the corner of the shrubbery, and there Conradin stationed himself. He saw the Woman enter, and then he imagined her opening the door of the sacred hutch and peering down with her short-sighted eyes into the thick straw bed where his god lay hidden. Perhaps she would prod at the straw in her clumsy impatience. And Conradin fervently breathed his prayer, for the last time. But he knew as he prayed that he did not believe. He knew that the Woman would come out presently with that pursed smile he loathed so well on her face, and that in an hour or two the gardener would carry away his wonderful god, a god no longer, but a simple brown ferret in a hutch. And he knew that the Woman would triumph always as she triumphed now, and that he would grow ever more sickly under her pestering and domineering and superior wisdom, till one day nothing would matter much more with him, and the doctor would be proved right. And in the sting and misery of his defeat, he began to chant loudly and defiantly the hymn of his threatened idol:

Sredni Vashtar went forth,
His thoughts were red thoughts and his teeth were white.
His enemies called for peace, but he brought them death.
Sredni Vashtar the Beautiful.

And then of a sudden he stopped his chanting and drew closer to the window-pane. The door of the shed still stood ajar as it had been left, and the minutes were slipping by. They were long minutes, but they slipped by nevertheless. He watched the starlings running and flying in little parties across the lawn; he counted them over and over again, with one eye always on that swinging door. A sour-faced maid came in to lay the table for tea, and still Conradin stood and waited and watched. Hope had crept by inches into his heart, and now a look of triumph began to blaze in his eyes that had only known the wistful patience of defeat. Under his breath, with a furtive exultation, he began once again the pæan of victory and devastation. And presently his eyes were rewarded: out through that doorway came a long, low, yellow-and-brown beast, with eyes a-blink at the waning daylight, and dark wet stains around the fur of jaws and throat. Conradin dropped on his knees. The great polecat-ferret made its way down to a small brook at the foot of the garden, drank for a moment, then crossed a little plank bridge and was lost to sight in the bushes. Such was the passing of Sredni Vashtar.

'Tea is ready,' said the sour-faced maid; 'where is the mistress?'

'She went down to the shed some time ago,' said Conradin.

And while the maid went to summon her mistress to tea, Conradin fished a toasting-fork out of the sideboard drawer and proceeded to toast himself a piece of bread. And during the toasting of it and the buttering of it with much butter and the slow enjoyment of eating it, Conradin listened to the noises and silences which fell in quick spasms beyond the dining-room door. The loud foolish screaming of the maid, the answering chorus of wondering ejaculations from the kitchen region, the scuttering footsteps and hurried embassies for outside help, and then, after a lull, the scared sobbings and the shuffling tread of those who bore a heavy burden into the house.

'Whoever will break it to the poor child? I couldn't for the life of me!' exclaimed a shrill voice. And while they debated the matter among themselves, Conradin made himself another piece of toast.

ADRIAN

A CHAPTER IN ACCLIMATIZATION

His baptismal register spoke of him pessimistically as John
Henry, but he had left that behind with the other maladies of
infancy, and his friends knew him under the front-name of
Adrian. His mother lived in Bethnal Green, which was not
altogether his fault; one can discourage too much history in
one's family, but one cannot always prevent geography. And,
after all, the Bethnal Green habit has this virtue—that it is
seldom transmitted to the next generation. Adrian lived in a
roomlet which came under the auspicious constellation of W.

How he lived was to a great extent a mystery even to himself; his struggle for existence probably coincided in many
material details with the rather dramatic accounts he gave of it
to sympathetic acquaintances. All that is definitely known is
that he now and then emerged from the struggle to dine at the
Ritz or Carlton, correctly garbed and with a correctly critical
appetite. On these occasions he was usually the guest of
Lucas Croyden, an amiable worldling, who had three thousand
a year and a taste for introducing impossible people to irre-
proachable cookery. Like most men who combine three
thousand a year with an uncertain digestion, Lucas was a
Socialist, and he argued that you cannot hope to elevate the
masses until you have brought plovers' eggs into their lives
and taught them to appreciate the difference between coupe
Jacques and Macédoine de fruits. His friends pointed out that
it was a doubtful kindness to initiate a boy from behind a
drapery counter into the blessedness of the higher catering, to
which Lucas invariably replied that all kindnesses were doubtful.
Which was perhaps true.

It was after one of his Adrian evenings that Lucas met his
aunt, Mrs. Mebberley, at a fashionable tea-shop, where the lamp

of family life is still kept burning and you meet relatives who might otherwise have slipped your memory.

'Who was that good-looking boy who was dining with you last night?' she asked. 'He looked much too nice to be thrown away upon you.'

Susan Mebberley was a charming woman, but she was also an aunt.

'Who are his people?' she continued, when the protégé's name (revised version) had been given her.

'His mother lives at Beth——'

Lucas checked himself on the threshold of what was perhaps a social indiscretion.

'Beth? Where is it? It sounds like Asia Minor. Is she mixed up with Consular people?'

'Oh, no. Her work lies among the poor.'

This was a side-slip into truth. The mother of Adrian was employed in a laundry.

'I see,' said Mrs. Mebberley, 'mission work of some sort. And meanwhile the boy has no one to look after him. It's obviously my duty to see that he doesn't come to harm. Bring him to call on me."

'My dear Aunt Susan,' expostulated Lucas, 'I really know very little about him. He may not be at all nice, you know, on further acquaintance.'

'He has delightful hair and a weak mouth. I shall take him with me to Homburg or Cairo.'

'It's the maddest thing I ever heard of,' said Lucas angrily.

'Well, there is a strong strain of madness in our family. If you haven't noticed it yourself all your friends must have.'

'One is so dreadfully under everybody's eyes at Homburg. At least you might give him a preliminary trial at Etretat.'

'And be surrounded by Americans trying to talk French? No, thank you. I love Americans, but not when they try to talk French. What a blessing it is that they never try to talk English. To-morrow at five you can bring your young friend to call on me."

And Lucas, realizing that Susan Mebberley was a woman as well as an aunt, saw that she would have to be allowed to have her own way.

Adrian was duly carried abroad under the Mebberley wing; but as a reluctant concession to sanity Homburg and other inconveniently fashionable resorts were given a wide berth, and the Mebberley establishment planted itself down in the best hotel at Dohledorf, an Alpine townlet somewhere at the back of the Engadine.   It was the usual kind of resort, with the usual type of visitors, that one finds over the greater part of Switzerland during the summer season, but to Adrian it was all unusual. The mountain air, the certainty of regular and abundant meals, and in particular the social atmosphere, affected him much as the indiscriminating fervour of a forcing-house might affect a weed that had strayed within its limits.   He had been brought up in a world where breakages were regarded as crimes and expiated as such; it was something new and altogether exhilarating to find that you were considered rather amusing if you smashed things in the right manner and at the recognized hours.   Susan Mebberley had expressed the intention of showing Adrian a bit of the world; the particular bit of the world represented by Dohledorf began to be shown a good deal of Adrian.

Lucas got occasional glimpses of the Alpine sojourn, not from his aunt or Adrian, but from the industrious pen of Clovis, who was also moving as a satellite in the Mebberley constellation.

' The entertainment which Susan got up last night ended in disaster.   I thought it would.   The Grobmayer child, a particularly loathsome five-year-old, had appeared as " Bubbles " during the early part of the evening, and been put to bed during the interval.   Adrian watched his opportunity and kidnapped it when the nurse was downstairs, and introduced it during the second half of the entertainment, thinly disguised as a performing pig.   It certainly *looked* very like a pig, and grunted and slobbered just like the real article ; no one knew exactly what it was, but every one said it was awfully clever, especially the Grobmayers.   At the third curtain Adrian pinched it too hard, and it yelled " Marmar "!   I am supposed to be good at descriptions, but don't ask me to describe the sayings and doings of the Grobmayers at that moment; it was like one of the angrier Psalms set to Strauss's music.   We have moved to an hotel higher up the valley.'

Clovis's next letter arrived five days later, and was written from the Hotel Steinbock.

' We left the Hotel Victoria this morning.   It was fairly comfortable and quiet—at least there was an air of repose about it when we arrived.   Before we had been in residence twenty-four hours most of the repose had vanished " like a dutiful bream," as Adrian expressed it.   However, nothing unduly outrageous happened till last night, when Adrian had a fit of insomnia and amused himself by unscrewing and transposing all the bedroom numbers on his floor.   He transferred the bathroom label to the adjoining bedroom door, which happened to be that of Frau Hofrath Schilling, and this morning from seven o'clock onwards the old lady had a stream of involuntary visitors;   she was too horrified and scandalized it seems to get up and lock her door.   The would-be bathers flew back in confusion to their rooms, and, of course, the change of numbers led them astray again, and the corridor gradually filled with panic-stricken, scantily robed humans, dashing wildly about like rabbits in a ferret-infested warren.   It took nearly an hour before the guests were all sorted into their respective rooms, and the Frau Hofrath's condition was still causing some anxiety when we left.   Susan is beginning to look a little worried.   She can't very well turn the boy adrift, as he hasn't got any money, and she can't send him to his people as she doesn't know where they are.   Adrian says his mother moves about a good deal and he's lost her address.   Probably, if the truth were known, he's had a row at home.   So many boys nowadays seem to think that quarrelling with one's family is a recognized occupation.'

Lucas's next communication from the travellers took the form of a telegram from Mrs. Mebberley herself. It was sent 'reply prepaid,' and consisted of a single sentence: 'In Heaven's name, where is Beth?'

THE CHAPLET

A STRANGE stillness hung over the restaurant; it was one of those rare moments when the orchestra was not discoursing the strains of the Ice-cream Sailor waltz.

'Did I ever tell you,' asked Clovis of his friend, 'the tragedy of music at mealtimes?

'It was a gala evening at the Grand Sybaris Hotel, and a special dinner was being served in the Amethyst dining-hall. The Amethyst dining-hall had almost a European reputation, especially with that section of Europe which is historically identified with the Jordan Valley. Its cooking was beyond reproach, and its orchestra was sufficiently highly salaried to be above criticism. Thither came in shoals the intensely musical and the almost intensely musical, who are very many, and in still greater numbers the merely musical, who know how Tchaikowsky's name is pronounced and can recognize several of Chopin's nocturnes if you give them due warning; these eat in the nervous, detached manner of roebuck feeding in the open, and keep anxious ears cocked towards the orchestra for the first hint of a recognizable melody.

'"Ah, yes, Pagliacci," they murmur, as the opening strains follow hot upon the soup, and if no contradiction is forthcoming from any better-informed quarter they break forth into subdued humming by way of supplementing the efforts of the musicians. Sometimes the melody starts on level terms with the soup, in which case the banqueters contrive somehow to hum between the spoonfuls; the facial expression of enthusiasts who are punctuating Potage St. Germain with Pagliacci is not beautiful, but it should be seen by those who are bent on observing all sides of life. One cannot discount the unpleasant things of this world merely by looking the other way.

'In addition to the aforementioned types the restaurant was patronized by a fair sprinkling of the absolutely non-musical;

62

their presence in the dining-hall could only be explained on the supposition that they had come there to dine.

" The earlier stages of the dinner had worn off. The wine lists had been consulted, by some with the blank embarrassment of a schoolboy suddenly called on to locate a Minor Prophet in the tangled hinterland of the Old Testament, by others with the severe scrutiny which suggests that they have visited most of the higher-priced wines in their own homes and probed their family weaknesses. The diners who chose their wine in the latter fashion always gave their orders in a penetrating voice, with a plentiful garnishing of stage directions. By insisting on having your bottle pointing to the north when the cork is being drawn, and calling the waiter Max, you may induce an impression on your guests which hours of laboured boasting might be powerless to achieve. For this purpose, however, the guests must be chosen as carefully as the wine.

' Standing aside from the revellers in the shadow of a massive pillar was an interested spectator who was assuredly of the feast, and yet not in it. Monsieur Aristide Saucourt was the *chef* of the Grand Sybaris Hotel, and if he had an equal in his profession he had never acknowledged the fact. In his own domain he was a potentate, hedged around with the cold brutality that Genius expects rather than excuses in her children; he never forgave, and those who served him were careful that there should be little to forgive. In the outer world, the world which devoured his creations, he was an influence; how profound or how shallow an influence he never attempted to guess. It is the penalty and the safeguard of genius that it computes itself by troy weight in a world that measures by vulgar hundredweights.

' Once in a way the great man would be seized with a desire to watch the effect of his master-efforts, just as the guiding brain of Krupp's might wish at a supreme moment to intrude into the firing line of an artillery duel. And such an occasion was the present. For the first time in the history of the Grand Sybaris Hotel, he was presenting to its guests the dish which he had brought to that pitch of perfection which almost amounts to scandal. Canetons à la mode d'Amblève. In thin gilt lettering on the creamy white of the menu how little those words conveyed to the bulk of the imperfectly educated diners. And yet how much specialized effort had been lavished, how much carefully treasured lore had been ungarnered, before those six words could be written. In the Department of Deux-Sèvres ducklings had lived peculiar and beautiful lives and died in the odour of satiety to furnish the main theme of the dish; champignons, which even a purist for Saxon English would have hesitated to address as mushrooms, had contributed their languorous atrophied bodies to the garnishing, and a sauce devised in the twilight reign of the Fifteenth Louis had been summoned back from the imperishable past to take its part in the wonderful confection. Thus far had human effort laboured to achieve the desired result; the rest had been left to human genius—the genius of Aristide Saucourt.

' And now the moment had arrived for the serving of the great dish, the dish which world-weary Grand Dukes and market-obsessed money magnates counted among their happiest memories. And at the same moment something else happened. The leader of the highly salaried orchestra placed his violin caressingly against his chin, lowered his eyelids, and floated into a sea of melody.

' " Hark ! " said most of the diners, " he is playing ' The Chaplet.' "

' They knew it was " The Chaplet " because they had heard it played at luncheon and afternoon tea, and at supper the night before, and had not had time to forget.

' " Yes, he is playing ' The Chaplet,' " they reassured one another. The general voice was unanimous on the subject. The orchestra had already played it eleven times that day, four times by desire and seven times from force of habit, but the familiar strains were greeted with the rapture due to a revelation. A murmur of much humming rose from half the tables in the room, and some of the more overwrought listeners laid down knife and fork in order to be able to burst in with loud clappings at the earliest permissible moment.

'And the Canetons à la mode d'Amblève? In stupefied, sickened wonder Aristide watched them grow cold in total neglect, or suffer the almost worse indignity of perfunctory pecking and listless munching while the banqueters lavished their approval and applause on the music-makers. Calves' liver and bacon, with parsley sauce, could hardly have figured more ignominiously in the evening's entertainment. And while the master of culinary art leaned back against the sheltering pillar, choking with a horrible brain-searing rage that could find no out-let for its agony, the orchestra leader was bowing his acknow-ledgments of the hand-clappings that rose in a storm around him. Turning to his colleagues he nodded the signal for an encore. But before the violin had been lifted anew into position there came from the shadow of the pillar an explosive negative.

' "Noh! Noh! You do not play thot again!"

'The musician turned in furious astonishment. Had he taken warning from the look in the other man's eyes he might have acted differently. But the admiring plaudits were ringing in his ears, and he snarled out sharply, "That is for me to decide."

' "Noh! You play thot never again," shouted the *chef*, and the next moment he had flung himself violently upon the loathed being who had supplanted him in the world's esteem. A large metal tureen, filled to the brim with steaming soup, had just been placed on a side table in readiness for a late party of diners; before the waiting staff or the guests had time to realize what was happening, Aristide had dragged his struggling victim up to the table and plunged his head deep down into the almost boiling contents of the tureen. At the further end of the room the diners were still spasmodically applauding in view of an encore.

'Whether the leader of the orchestra died from drowning by soup, or from the shock to his professional vanity, or was scalded to death, the doctors were never wholly able to agree. Monsieur Aristide Saucourt, who now lives in complete retire-ment, always inclined to the drowning theory.'

C (547)

THE QUEST

An unwonted peace hung over the Villa Elsinore, broken, however, at frequent intervals, by clamorous lamentations sugges-
tive of bewildered bereavement.   The Momebys had lost
their infant child; hence the peace which its absence entailed;
they were looking for it in wild, undisciplined fashion, giving
tongue the whole time, which accounted for the outcry which
swept through house and garden whenever they returned to
try the home coverts anew.   Clovis, who was temporarily
and unwillingly a paying guest at the villa, had been dozing in
a hammock at the far end of the garden when Mrs. Momeby
had broken the news to him.

'We've lost Baby,' she screamed.

'Do you mean that it's dead, or stampeded, or that you
staked it at cards and lost it that way?' asked Clovis lazily.

'He was toddling about quite happily on the lawn,' said
Mrs. Momeby tearfully, 'and Arnold had just come in, and I
was asking him what sort of sauce he would like with the
asparagus——'

'I hope he said hollandaise,' interrupted Clovis, with a show
of quickened interest, 'because if there's anything I hate——'

'And all of a sudden I missed Baby,' continued Mrs. Momeby
in a shriller tone.   'We've hunted high and low, in house and
garden and outside the gates, and he's nowhere to be seen.'

'Is he anywhere to be heard?' asked Clovis; 'if not, he
must be at least two miles away.'

'But where?   And how?' asked the distracted mother.

'Perhaps an eagle or a wild beast has carried him off,'
suggested Clovis.

'There aren't eagles and wild beasts in Surrey,' said Mrs.
Momeby, but a note of horror had crept into her voice.

'They escape now and then from travelling shows.   Some-
tmies I think they let them get loose for the sake of the advertise-

66

ment.   Think what a sensational headline it would make in the local papers: " Infant son of prominent Nonconformist devoured by spotted hyæna."   Your husband isn't a prominent Nonconformist, but his mother came of Wesleyan stock, and you must allow the newspapers some latitude.'

' But we should have found his remains,' sobbed Mrs. Momeby.

' If the hyæna was really hungry and not merely toying with his food there wouldn't be much in the way of remains.   It would be like the small-boy-and-apple story—there ain't going to be no core.'

Mrs. Momeby turned away hastily to seek comfort and counsel in some other direction.   With the selfish absorption of young motherhood she entirely disregarded Clovis's obvious anxiety about the asparagus sauce.   Before she had gone a yard, however, the click of the side gate caused her to pull up sharp.   Miss Gilpet, from the Villa Peterhof, had come over to hear details of the bereavement.   Clovis was already rather bored with the story, but Mrs. Momeby was equipped with that merciless faculty which finds as much joy in the ninetieth time of telling as in the first.

' Arnold had just come in; he was complaining of rheumatism——'

' There are so many things to complain of in this household that it would never have occurred to me to complain of rheumatism,' murmured Clovis.

' He was complaining of rheumatism,' continued Mrs. Momeby, trying to throw a chilling inflection into a voice that was already doing a good deal of sobbing and talking at high pressure as well.

She was again interrupted.

' There is no such thing as rheumatism,' said Miss Gilpet. She said it with the conscious air of defiance that a waiter adopts in announcing that the cheapest-priced claret in the wine-list is no more.   She did not proceed, however, to offer the alternative of some more expensive malady, but denied the existence of them all.

Mrs. Momeby's temper began to shine out through her grief.

' I suppose you'll say next that Baby hasn't really disappeared.'

' He has disappeared,' conceded Miss Gilpet, ' but only because you haven't sufficient faith to find him.   It's only lack of faith on your part that prevents him from being restored to you safe and well.'

' But if he's been eaten in the meantime by a hyæna and partly digested,' said Clovis, who clung affectionately to his wild beast theory, ' surely some ill-effects would be noticeable ? '

Miss Gilpet was rather staggered by this complication of the question.

' I feel sure that a hyæna has not eaten him,' she said lamely.

' The hyæna may be equally certain that it has.   You see it may have just as much faith as you have, and more special knowledge as to the present whereabouts of the baby.'

Mrs. Momeby was in tears again.   ' If you have faith,' she sobbed, struck by a happy inspiration, ' won't you find our little Erik for us?   I am sure you have powers that are denied to us.'

Rose-Marie Gilpet was thoroughly sincere in her adherence to Christian Science principles; whether she understood or correctly expounded them the learned in such matters may best decide.   In the present case she was undoubtedly confronted with a great opportunity, and as she started forth on her vague search she strenuously summoned to her aid every scrap of faith that she possessed.   She passed out into the bare and open high road, followed by Mrs. Momeby's warning, ' It's no use going there, we've searched there a dozen times.'   But Rose-Marie's ears were already deaf to all things save self-congratulation; for sitting in the middle of the highway, playing contentedly with the dust and some faded buttercups, was a white-pinafored baby with a mop of tow-coloured hair tied over one temple with a pale-blue ribbon.   Taking first the usual feminine precaution of looking to see that no motor-car was on the distant horizon, Rose-Marie dashed at the child and bore it, despite its vigorous opposition, in through the portals of Elsinore. The child's furious screams had already announced the fact of its discovery, and the almost hysterical parents raced down the lawn to meet their restored offspring. The æsthetic value of the scene was marred in some degree by Rose-Marie's difficulty in holding the struggling infant, which was borne wrong-end foremost towards the agitated bosom of its family. 'Our own little Erik come back to us,' cried the Momebys in unison; as the child had rammed its fists tightly into its eye-sockets and nothing could be seen of its face but a widely gaping mouth, the recognition was in itself almost an act of faith.

'Is he glad to get back to Daddy and Mummy again?' crooned Mrs Momeby; the preference which the child was showing for its dust and buttercup distractions was so marked that the question struck Clovis as being unnecessarily tactless.

'Give him a ride on the roly-poly,' suggested the father brilliantly, as the howls continued with no sign of early abatement. In a moment the child had been placed astride the big garden roller and a preliminary tug was given to set it in motion. From the hollow depths of the cylinder came an ear-splitting roar, drowning even the vocal efforts of the squalling baby, and immediately afterwards there crept forth a white-pinafored infant with a mop of tow-coloured hair tied over one temple with a pale blue ribbon. There was no mistaking either the features or the lung-power of the new arrival.

'Our own little Erik,' screamed Mrs. Momeby, pouncing on him and nearly smothering him with kisses; 'did he hide in the roly-poly to give us all a big fright?'

This was the obvious explanation of the child's sudden disappearance and equally abrupt discovery. There remained, however, the problem of the interloping baby, which now sat whimpering on the lawn in a disfavour as chilling as its previous popularity had been unwelcome. The Momebys glared at it as though it had wormed its way into their short-lived affections by heartless and unworthy pretences. Miss Gilpet's face took on an ashen tinge as she stared helplessly at the bunched-up figure that had been such a gladsome sight to her eyes a few moments ago.

'When love is over, how little of love even the lover understands,' quoted Clovis to himself.

Rose-Marie was the first to break the silence.

'If that is Erik you have in your arms, who is—that?'

'That, I think, is for you to explain,' said Mrs. Momeby stiffly.

'Obviously,' said Clovis, 'it's a duplicate Erik that your powers of faith called into being. The question is: What are you going to do with him?'

The ashen pallor deepened in Rose-Marie's cheeks. Mrs. Momeby clutched the genuine Erik closer to her side, as though she feared that her uncanny neighbour might out of sheer pique turn him into a bowl of gold-fish.

'I found him sitting in the middle of the road,' said Rose-Marie weakly.

'You can't take him back and leave him there,' said Clovis; 'the highway is meant for traffic, not to be used as a lumber-room for disused miracles.'

Rose-Marie wept. The proverb 'Weep and you weep alone,' broke down as badly on application as most of its kind. Both babies were wailing lugubriously, and the parent Momebys had scarcely recovered from their earlier lachrymose condition. Clovis alone maintained an unruffled cheerfulness.

'Must I keep him always?' asked Rose-Marie dolefully.

'Not always,' said Clovis consolingly; 'he can go into the Navy when he's thirteen.' Rose-Marie wept afresh.

'Of course,' added Clovis, 'there may be no end of a bother about his birth certificate. You'll have to explain matters to the Admiralty, and they're dreadfully hidebound.'

It was rather a relief when a breathless nursemaid from the Villa Charlottenburg over the way came running across the lawn to claim little Percy, who had slipped out of the front gate and disappeared like a twinkling from the high road.

And even then Clovis found it necessary to go in person to the kitchen to make sure about the asparagus sauce.

WRATISLAV

THE Gräfin's two elder sons had made deplorable marriages. It was, observed Clovis, a family habit. The youngest boy, Wratislav, who was the black sheep of a rather greyish family, had as yet made no marriage at all.

' There is certainly this much to be said for viciousness,' said the Gräfin, ' it keeps boys out of mischief.'

' Does it?' asked the Baroness Sophie, not by way of questioning the statement, but with a painstaking effort to talk intelligently. It was the one matter in which she attempted to override the decrees of Providence, which had obviously never intended that she should talk otherwise than inanely.

' I don't know why I shouldn't talk cleverly,' she would complain; ' my mother was considered a brilliant conversationalist.'

' These things have a way of skipping one generation,' said the Gräfin.

' That seems so unjust,' said Sophie; ' one doesn't object to one's mother having outshone one as a clever talker, but I must admit that I should be rather annoyed if my daughters talked brilliantly.'

' Well, none of them do,' said the Gräfin consolingly.

' I don't know about that,' said the Baroness, promptly veering round in defence of her offspring. ' Elsa said something quite clever on Thursday about the Triple Alliance. Something about it being like a paper umbrella, that was all right as long as you didn't take it out in the rain. It's not every one who could say that.'

' Every one has said it; at least every one that I know. But then I know very few people.'

' I don't think you're particularly agreeable to-day.'

' I never am. Haven't you noticed that women with a really perfect profile like mine are seldom even moderately agreeable?'

'I don't think your profile is so perfect as all that,' said the Baroness.

'It would be surprising if it wasn't.   My mother was one of the most noted classical beauties of her day.'

'These things sometimes skip a generation, you know,' put in the Baroness, with the breathless haste of one to whom repartee comes as rarely as the finding of a gold-handled umbrella.

'My dear Sophie,' said the Gräfin sweetly, 'that isn't in the least bit clever; but you do try so hard that I suppose I oughtn't to discourage you.   Tell me something: has it ever occurred to you that Elsa would do very well for Wratislav?   It's time he married somebody, and why not Elsa?'

'Elsa marry that dreadful boy!' gasped the Baroness.

'Beggars can't be choosers,' observed the Gräfin.

'Elsa isn't a beggar!'

'Not financially, or I shouldn't have suggested the match. But she's getting on, you know, and has no pretensions to brains or looks or anything of that sort.'

'You seem to forget that she's my daughter.'

'That shows my generosity.   But, seriously, I don't see what there is against Wratislav.   He has no debts—at least, nothing worth speaking about.'

'But think of his reputation!   If half the things they say about him are true——'

'Probably three-quarters of them are.   But what of it? You don't want an archangel for a son-in-law.'

'I don't want Wratislav.   My poor Elsa would be miserable with him.'

'A little misery wouldn't matter very much with her; it would go so well with the way she does her hair, and if she couldn't get on with Wratislav she could always go and do good among the poor.'

The Baroness picked up a framed photograph from the table.

'He certainly is very handsome,' she said doubtfully; adding even more doubtfully, 'I dare say dear Elsa might reform him.'

The Gräfin had the presence of mind to laugh in the right key.

* * *

Three weeks later the Gräfin bore down upon the Baroness Sophie in a foreign bookseller's shop in the Graben, where she was, possibly, buying books of devotion, though it was the wrong counter for them.

'I've just left the dear children at the Rodenstahls',' was the Gräfin's greeting.

'Were they looking very happy?' asked the Baroness.

'Wratislav was wearing some new English clothes, so, of course, he was quite happy. I overheard him telling Toni a rather amusing story about a nun and a mousetrap, which won't bear repetition. Elsa was telling every one else a witticism about the Triple Alliance being like a paper umbrella—which seems to bear repetition with Christian fortitude.'

'Did they seem much wrapped up in each other?'

'To be candid, Elsa looked as if she were wrapped up in a horse-rug. And why let her wear saffron colour?'

'I always think it goes with her complexion.'

'Unfortunately it doesn't. It stays with it. Ugh. Don't forget, you're lunching with me on Thursday.'

The Baroness was late for her luncheon engagement the following Thursday.

'Imagine what has happened!' she screamed as she burst into the room.

'Something remarkable, to make you late for a meal,' said the Gräfin.

'Elsa has run away with the Rodenstahls' chauffeur!'

'Kolossal!'

'Such a thing as that no one in our family has ever done,' gasped the Baroness.

'Perhaps he didn't appeal to them in the same way,' suggested the Gräfin judicially.

The Baroness began to feel that she was not getting the astonishment and sympathy to which her catastrophe entitled her.

' At any rate,' she snapped, ' now she can't marry Wratislav.'

' She couldn't in any case,' said the Gräfin; ' he left suddenly for abroad last night.'

' For abroad! Where?'

' For Mexico, I believe.'

' Mexico! But what for? Why Mexico?'

' The English have a proverb, " Conscience makes cowboys of us all." '

' I didn't know Wratislav had a conscience.'

' My dear Sophie, he hasn't. It's other people's consciences that send one abroad in a hurry. Let's go and eat.'

THE EASTER EGG

It was distinctly hard lines for Lady Barbara, who came of good fighting stock, and was one of the bravest women of her generation, that her son should be so undisguisedly a coward. Whatever good qualities Lester Slaggby may have possessed, and he was in some respects charming, courage could certainly never be imputed to him. As a child he had suffered from childish timidity, as a boy from unboyish funk, and as a youth he had exchanged unreasoning fears for others which were more formidable from the fact of having a carefully-thought-out basis. He was frankly afraid of animals, nervous with firearms, and never crossed the Channel without mentally comparing the numerical proportion of lifebelts to passengers. On horseback he seemed to require as many hands as a Hindu god, at least four for clutching the reins, and two more for patting the horse soothingly on the neck. Lady Barbara no longer pretended not to see her son's prevailing weakness; with her usual courage she faced the knowledge of it squarely, and, motherlike, loved him none the less.

Continental travel, anywhere away from the great tourist tracks, was a favoured hobby with Lady Barbara, and Lester joined her as often as possible. Eastertide usually found her at Knobaltheim, an upland township in one of those small princedoms that make inconspicuous freckles on the map of Central Europe.

A long-standing acquaintanceship with the reigning family made her a personage of due importance in the eyes of her old friend the Burgomaster, and she was anxiously consulted by that worthy on the momentous occasion when the Prince made known his intention of coming in person to open a sanatorium outside the town. All the usual items in a programme of welcome, some of them fatuous and commonplace, others quaint and charming, had been arranged for, but the Burgomaster hoped

that the resourceful English lady might have something new
and tasteful to suggest in the way of loyal greeting. The
Prince was known to the outside world, if at all, as an old-
fashioned reàctionary, combating modern progress, as it were,
with a wooden sword; to his own people he was known as a
kindly old gentleman with a certain endearing stateliness which
had nothing of standoffishness about it. Knobaltheim was
anxious to do its best. Lady Barbara discussed the matter
with Lester and one or two acquaintances in her little hotel, but
ideas were difficult to come by.

' Might I suggest something to the Gnädige Frau?' asked a
sallow high-cheek-boned lady to whom the Englishwoman had
spoken once or twice, and whom she had set down in her mind
as probably a Southern Slav.

' Might I suggest something for the Reception Fest?' she
went on, with a certain shy eagerness.   ' Our little child here,
our baby, we will dress him in little white coat, with small
wings, as an Easter angel, and he will carry a large white Easter
egg, and inside shall be a basket of plover eggs, of which the
Prince is so fond, and he shall give it to his Highness as Easter
offering.   It is so pretty an idea; we have seen it done once in
Styria.'

Lady Barbara looked dubiously at the proposed Easter angel,
a fair, wooden-faced child of about four years old. She had
noticed it the day before in the hotel, and wondered rather
how such a tow-headed child could belong to such a dark-
visaged couple as the woman and her husband; probably, she
thought, an adopted baby, especially as the couple were not
young.

' Of course Gnädige Frau will escort the little child up to the
Prince,' pursued the woman; ' but he will be quite good, and
do as he is told.'

' We haf some pluffers' eggs shall come fresh from Wien,'
said the husband.

The small child and Lady Barbara seemed equally unen-
thusiastic about the pretty idea; Lester was openly discourag-

ing, but when the Burgomaster heard of it he was enchanted. The combination of sentiment and plovers' eggs appealed strongly to his Teutonic mind.

On the eventful day the Easter angel, really quite prettily and quaintly dressed, was a centre of kindly interest to the gala crowd marshalled to receive his Highness. The mother was unobtrusive and less fussy than most parents would have been under the circumstances, merely stipulating that she should place the Easter egg herself in the arms that had been carefully schooled how to hold the precious burden. Then Lady Barbara moved forward, the child marching stolidly and with grim determination at her side. It had been promised cakes and sweeties galore if it gave the egg well and truly to the kind old gentleman who was waiting to receive it. Lester had tried to convey to it privately that horrible smackings would attend any failure in its share of the proceedings, but it is doubtful if his German caused more than an immediate distress. Lady Barbara had thoughtfully provided herself with an emergency supply of chocolate sweetmeats; children may sometimes be time-servers, but they do not encourage long accounts. As they approached nearer to the princely daïs Lady Barbara stood discreetly aside, and the stolid-faced infant walked forward alone, with staggering but steadfast gait, encouraged by a murmur of elderly approval. Lester, standing in the front row of the onlookers, turned to scan the crowd for the beaming faces of the happy parents. In a side-road which led to the railway station he saw a cab; entering the cab with every appearance of furtive haste were the dark-visaged couple who had been so plausibly eager for the ' pretty idea.' The sharpened instinct of cowardice lit up the situation to him in one swift flash. The blood roared and surged to his head as though thousands of floodgates had been opened in his veins and arteries, and his brain was the common sluice in which all the torrents met. He saw nothing but a blur around him. Then the blood ebbed away in quick waves, till his very heart seemed drained and empty, and he stood nervelessly, helplessly, dumbly watching the child, bearing its accursed burden with slow, relentless steps nearer and nearer to the group that waited sheep-like to receive him. A fascinated curiosity compelled Lester to turn his head towards the fugitives; the cab had started at hot pace in the direction of the station.

The next moment Lester was running, running faster than any of those present had ever seen a man run, and—he was not running away. For that stray fraction of his life some unwonted impulse beset him, some hint of the stock he came from, and he ran unflinchingly towards danger. He stooped and clutched at the Easter egg as one tries to scoop up the ball in Rugby football. What he meant to do with it he had not considered, the thing was to get it. But the child had been promised cakes and sweetmeats if it safely gave the egg into the hands of the kindly old gentleman; it uttered no scream, but it held to its charge with limpet grip. Lester sank to his knees, tugging savagely at the tightly clasped burden, and angry cries rose from the scandalized onlookers. A questioning, threatening ring formed round him, then shrank back in recoil as he shrieked out one hideous word. Lady Barbara heard the word and saw the crowd race away like scattered sheep, saw the Prince forcibly hustled away by his attendants, also she saw her son lying prone in an agony of overmastering terror, his spasm of daring shattered by the child's unexpected resistance, still clutching frantically, as though for safety, at that white-satin gew-gaw, unable to crawl even from its deadly neighbourhood, able only to scream and scream and scream. In her brain she was dimly conscious of balancing, or striving to balance, the abject shame which had him now in thrall against the one compelling act of courage which had flung him grandly and madly on to the point of danger. It was only for the fraction of a minute that she stood watching the two entangled figures, the infant with its woodenly obstinate face and body tense with dogged resistance, and the boy limp and already nearly dead with a terror that almost stifled his screams; and over them the long gala streamers flapping gaily in the sunshine.

She never forget the scene; but then, it was the last she ever saw.

Lady Barbara carries her scarred face with its sightless eyes as bravely as ever in the world, but at Eastertide her friends are careful to keep from her ears any mention of the Children's Easter symbol.

FILBOID STUDGE, THE STORY OF A MOUSE THAT HELPED

'I WANT to marry your daughter,' said Mark Spayley with faltering eagerness. 'I am only an artist with an income of two hundred a year, and she is the daughter of an enormously wealthy man, so I suppose you will think my offer a piece of presumption.'

Duncan Dullamy, the great company inflator, showed no outward sign of displeasure. As a matter of fact, he was secretly relieved at the prospect of finding even a two-hundred-a-year husband for his daughter Leonore. A crisis was rapidly rushing upon him, from which he knew he would emerge with neither money nor credit; all his recent ventures had fallen flat, and flattest of all had gone the wonderful new breakfast food, Pipenta, on the advertisement of which he had sunk such huge sums. It could scarcely be called a drug in the market; people bought drugs, but no one bought Pipenta.

'Would you marry Leonore if she were a poor man's daughter?' asked the man of phantom wealth.

'Yes,' said Mark, wisely avoiding the error of over-protestation. And to his astonishment Leonore's father not only gave his consent, but suggested a fairly early date for the wedding.

'I wish I could show my gratitude in some way,' said Mark with genuine emotion. 'I'm afraid it's rather like the mouse proposing to help the lion.'

'Get people to buy that beastly muck,' said Dullamy, nodding savagely at a poster of the despised Pipenta, 'and you'll have done more than any of my agents have been able to accomplish.'

'It wants a better name,' said Mark reflectively, 'and something distinctive in the poster line. Anyway, I'll have a shot at it.'

Three weeks later the world was advised of the coming of a

new breakfast food, heralded under the resounding name of
'Filboid Studge.'   Spayley put forth no pictures of massive
babies springing up with fungus-like rapidity under its forcing
influence, or of representatives of the leading nations of the
world scrambling with fatuous eagerness for its possession.
One huge sombre poster depicted the Damned in Hell suffering
a new torment from their inability to get at the Filboid Studge
which elegant young fiends held in transparent bowls just
beyond their reach.   The scene was rendered even more
gruesome by a subtle suggestion of the features of leading men
and women of the day in the portrayal of the Lost Souls;
prominent individuals of both political parties, Society hostesses,
well-known dramatic authors and novelists, and distinguished
aeroplanists were dimly recognizable in that doomed throng;
noted lights of the musical-comedy stage flickered wanly in the
shades of the Inferno, smiling still from force of habit, but with
the fearsome smiling rage of baffled effort.   The poster bore
no fulsome allusions to the merits of the new breakfast food,
but a single grim statement ran in bold letters along its base:
'They cannot buy it now.'

Spayley had grasped the fact that people will do things from
a sense of duty which they would never attempt as a pleasure.
There are thousands of respectable middle-class men who, if
you found them unexpectedly in a Turkish bath, would explain
in all sincerity that a doctor had ordered them to take Turkish
baths; if you told them in return that you went there because
you liked it, they would stare in pained wonder at the frivolity
of your motive.   In the same way, whenever a massacre of
Armenians is reported from Asia Minor, every one assumes
that it has been carried out 'under orders' from somewhere or
another; no one seems to think that there are people who
might *like* to kill their neighbours now and then.

And so it was with the new breakfast food.   No one would
have eaten Filboid Studge as a pleasure, but the grim austerity
of its advertisement drove housewives in shoals to the grocers'
shops to clamour for an immediate supply.   In small kitchens

solemn pig-tailed daughters helped depressed mothers to perform the primitive ritual of its preparation.   On the breakfast-tables of cheerless parlours it was partaken of in silence.   Once the womenfolk discovered that it was thoroughly unpalatable, their zeal in forcing it on their households knew no bounds. ' You haven't eaten your Filboid Studge! ' would be screamed at the appetiteless clerk as he hurried weariedly from the break-fast-table, and his evening meal would be prefaced by a warmed-up mess which would be explained as ' your Filboid Studge that you didn't eat this morning.'   Those strange fanatics who ostentatiously mortify themselves, inwardly and outwardly, with health biscuits and health garments, battened aggressively on the new food.   Earnest spectacled young men devoured it on the steps of the National Liberal Club.   A bishop who did not believe in a future state preached against the poster, and a peer's daughter died from eating too much of the compound. A further advertisement was obtained when an infantry regiment mutinied and shot its officers rather than eat the nauseous mess; fortunately, Lord Birrell of Blatherstone, who was War Minister at the moment, saved the situation by his happy epigram, that ' Discipline to be effective must be optional.'

Filboid Studge had become a household word, but Dullamy wisely realized that it was not necessarily the last word in breakfast dietary; its supremacy would be challenged as soon as some yet more unpalatable food should be put on the market. There might even be a reaction in favour of something tasty and appetizing, and the Puritan austerity of the moment might be banished from domestic cookery.   At an opportune moment, therefore, he sold out his interests in the article which had brought him in colossal wealth at a critical juncture, and placed his financial reputation beyond the reach of cavil.   As for Leonore, who was now an heiress on a far greater scale than ever before, he naturally found her something a vast deal higher in the husband market than a two-hundred-a-year poster designer.   Mark Spayley, the brainmouse who had helped the financial lion with such untoward effect, was left to curse the day he produced the wonder-working poster.

'After all,' said Clovis, meeting him shortly afterwards at his club, ' you have this doubtful consolation, that 'tis not in mortals to countermand success.'

THE MUSIC ON THE HILL

SYLVIA SELTOUN ate her breakfast in the morning-room at Yessney with a pleasant sense of ultimate victory, such as a fervent Ironside might have permitted himself on the morrow of Worcester fight. She was scarcely pugnacious by temperament, but belonged to that more successful class of fighters who are pugnacious by circumstance. Fate had willed that her life should be occupied with a series of small struggles, usually with the odds slightly against her, and usually she had just managed to come through winning. And now she felt that she had brought her hardest and certainly her most important struggle to a successful issue. To have married Mortimer Seltoun, 'Dead Mortimer' as his more intimate enemies called him, in the teeth of the cold hostility of his family, and in spite of his unaffected indifference to women, was indeed an achievement that had needed some determination and adroitness to carry through; yesterday she had brought her victory to its concluding stage by wrenching her husband away from Town and its groups of satellite watering-places and 'settling him down,' in the vocabulary of her kind, in this remote wood-girt manor farm which was his country house.

'You will never get Mortimer to go,' his mother had said carpingly, 'but if he once goes he'll stay; Yessney throws almost as much a spell over him as Town does. One can understand what holds him to Town, but Yessney——' and the dowager had shrugged her shoulders.

There was a sombre almost savage wildness about Yessney that was certainly not likely to appeal to town-bred tastes, and Sylvia, notwithstanding her name, was accustomed to nothing much more sylvan than 'leafy Kensington.' She looked on the country as something excellent and wholesome in its way, which was apt to become troublesome if you encouraged it overmuch. Distrust of town-life had been a new thing with her, born of her marriage with Mortimer, and she had watched with satisfaction the gradual fading of what she called 'the Jermyn-street-look' in his eyes as the woods and heather of Yessney had closed in on them yesternight. Her will-power and strategy had prevailed; Mortimer would stay.

Outside the morning-room windows was a triangular slope of turf, which the indulgent might call a lawn, and beyond its low hedge of neglected fuchsia bushes a steeper slope of heather and bracken dropped down into cavernous combes overgrown with oak and yew. In its wild open savagery there seemed a stealthy linking of the joy of life with the terror of unseen things. Sylvia smiled complacently as she gazed with a School-of-Art appreciation at the landscape, and then of a sudden she almost shuddered.

'It is very wild,' she said to Mortimer, who had joined her; 'one could almost think that in such a place the worship of Pan had never quite died out.'

'The worship of Pan never has died out,' said Mortimer. 'Other newer gods have drawn aside his votaries from time to time, but he is the Nature-God to whom all must come back at last. He has been called the Father of all the Gods, but most of his children have been stillborn.'

Sylvia was religious in an honest vaguely devotional kind of way, and did not like to hear her beliefs spoken of as mere aftergrowths, but it was at least something new and hopeful to hear Dead Mortimer speak with such energy and conviction on any subject.

'You don't really believe in Pan?' she asked incredulously.

'I've been a fool in most things,' said Mortimer quietly, 'but I'm not such a fool as not to believe in Pan when I'm down here. And if you're wise you won't disbelieve in him too boastfully while you're in his country.'

It was not till a week later, when Sylvia had exhausted the attractions of the woodland walks round Yessney, that she ventured on a tour of inspection of the farm buildings. A farmyard suggested in her mind a scene of cheerful bustle, with churns and flails and smiling dairymaids, and teams of horses drinking knee-deep in duck-crowded ponds.   As she wandered among the gaunt grey buildings of Yessney manor farm her first impression was one of crushing stillness and desolation, as though she had happened on some lone deserted homestead long given over to owls and cobwebs; then came a sense of furtive watchful hostility, the same shadow of unseen things that seemed to lurk in the wooded combes and coppices.   From behind heavy doors and shuttered windows came the restless stamp of hoof or rasp of chain halter, and at times a muffled bellow from some stalled beast.   From a distant corner a shaggy dog watched her with intent unfriendly eyes; as she drew near it slipped quietly into its kennel, and slipped out again as noiselessly when she had passed by.   A few hens, questing for food under a rick, stole away under a gate at her approach.   Sylvia felt that if she had come across any human beings in this wilderness of barn and byre they would have fled wraith-like from her gaze.   At last, turning a corner quickly, she came upon a living thing that did not fly from her.   Astretch in a pool of mud was an enormous sow, gigantic beyond the town-woman's wildest computation of swine-flesh, and speedily alert to resent and if necessary repel the unwonted intrusion.   It was Sylvia's turn to make an unobtrusive retreat.   As she threaded her way past rickyards and cowsheds and long blank walls, she started suddenly at a strange sound—the echo of a boy's laughter, golden and equivocal.   Jan, the only boy employed on the farm, a tow-headed, wizen-faced yokel, was visibly at work on a potato clearing half-way up the nearest hill-side, and Mortimer, when questioned, knew of no other probable or possible begetter of the hidden mockery that had ambushed Sylvia's retreat.   The memory of that untraceable echo was added to her other impressions of a furtive sinister ' something ' that hung around Yessney.

Of Mortimer she saw very little; farm and woods and trout-streams seemed to swallow him up from dawn till dusk.   Once, following the direction she had seen him take in the morning, she came to an open space in a nut copse, further shut in by huge yew trees, in the centre of which stood a stone pedestal surmounted by a small bronze figure of a youthful Pan. It was a beautiful piece of workmanship, but her attention was chiefly held by the fact that a newly cut bunch of grapes had been placed as an offering at its feet. Grapes were none too plentiful at the manor house, and Sylvia snatched the bunch angrily from the pedestal. Contemptuous annoyance dominated her thoughts as she strolled slowly homeward, and then gave way to a sharp feeling of something that was very near fright; across a thick tangle of undergrowth a boy's face was scowling at her, brown and beautiful, with unutterably evil eyes. It was a lonely pathway, all pathways round Yessney were lonely for the matter of that, and she sped forward without waiting to give a closer scrutiny to this sudden apparition. It was not till she had reached the house that she discovered that she had dropped the bunch of grapes in her flight.

' I saw a youth in the wood to-day,' she told Mortimer that evening, ' brown-faced and rather handsome, but a scoundrel to look at. A gipsy lad, I suppose.'

' A reasonable theory,' said Mortimer, ' only there aren't any gipsies in these parts at present.'

' Then who was he?' asked Sylvia, and as Mortimer appeared to have no theory of his own, she passed on to recount her finding of the votive offering.

' I suppose it was your doing,' she observed; ' it's a harmless piece of lunacy, but people would think you dreadfully silly if they knew of it.'

' Did you meddle with it in any way?' asked Mortimer.

' I—I threw the grapes away. It seemed so silly,' said Sylvia, watching Mortimer's impassive face for a sign of annoyance.

' I don't think you were wise to do that,' he said reflectively. ' I've heard it said that the Wood Gods are rather horrible to those who molest them.'

' Horrible perhaps to those that believe in them, but you see I don't,' retorted Sylvia.

' All the same,' said Mortimer in his even, dispassionate tone, ' I should avoid the woods and orchards if I were you, and give a wide berth to the horned beasts on the farm.'

It was all nonsense, of course, but in that lonely wood-girt spot nonsense seemed able to rear a bastard brood of uneasiness.

' Mortimer,' said Sylvia suddenly, ' I think we will go back to Town some time soon.'

Her victory had not been so complete as she had supposed; it had carried her on to ground that she was already anxious to quit.

' I don't think you will ever go back to Town,' said Mortimer. He seemed to be paraphrasing his mother's prediction as to himself.

Sylvia noted with dissatisfaction and some self-contempt that the course of her next afternoon's ramble took her instinctively clear of the network of woods. As to the horned cattle, Mortimer's warning was scarcely needed, for she had always regarded them as of doubtful neutrality at the best: her imagination unsexed the most matronly dairy cows and turned them into bulls liable to ' see red ' at any moment. The ram who fed in the narrow paddock below the orchards she had adjudged, after ample and cautious probation, to be of docile temper; to-day, however, she decided to leave his docility untested, for the usually tranquil beast was roaming with every sign of restlessness from corner to corner of his meadow. A low, fitful piping, as of some reedy flute, was coming from the depth of a neighbouring copse, and there seemed to be some subtle connection between the animal's restless pacing and the wild music from the wood. Sylvia turned her steps in an upward direction and climbed the heatherclad slopes that stretched in rolling shoulders high above Yessney. She had left the piping notes behind her, but across the wooded combes at her feet the wind brought her another

kind of music, the straining bay of hounds in full chase. Yessney was just on the outskirts of the Devon-and-Somerset
country, and the hunted deer sometimes came that way. Sylvia
could presently see a dark body, breasting hill after hill, and
sinking again and again out of sight as he crossed the combes,
while behind him steadily swelled that relentless chorus, and
she grew tense with the excited sympathy that one feels for any
hunted thing in whose capture one is not directly interested.
And at last he broke through the outermost line of oak scrub
and fern and stood panting in the open, a fat September stag
carrying a well-furnished head. His obvious course was to
drop down to the brown pools of Undercombe, and thence
make his way towards the red deer's favoured sanctuary, the
sea. To Sylvia's surprise, however, he turned his head to the
upland slope and came lumbering resolutely onward over the
heather. 'It will be dreadful,' she thought, 'the hounds will
pull him down under my very eyes.' But the music of the
pack seemed to have died away for a moment, and in its place
she heard again that wild piping, which rose now on this side,
now on that, as though urging the failing stag to a final effort.
Sylvia stood well aside from his path, half hidden in a thick
growth of whortle bushes, and watched him swing stiffly
upward, his flanks dark with sweat, the coarse hair on his neck
showing light by contrast. The pipe music shrilled suddenly
around her, seeming to come from the bushes at her very feet,
and at the same moment the great beast slewed round and bore
directly down upon her. In an instant her pity for the hunted
animal was changed to wild terror at her own danger; the
thick heather roots mocked her scrambling efforts at flight, and
she looked frantically downward for a glimpse of oncoming
hounds. The huge antler spikes were within a few yards of
her, and in a flash of numbing fear she remembered Mortimer's
warning, to beware of horned beasts on the farm. And then
with a quick throb of joy she saw that she was not alone; a
human figure stood a few paces aside, knee-deep in the whortle
bushes.

' Drive it off! ' she shrieked.   But the figure made no answering movement.

The antlers drove straight at her breast, the acrid smell of the hunted animal was in her nostrils, but her eyes were filled with the horror of something she saw other than her oncoming death.   And in her ears rang the echo of a boy's laughter, golden and equivocal.

THE STORY OF ST. VESPALUUS

'TELL me a story,' said the Baroness, staring out despairingly at the rain; it was that light, apologetic sort of rain that looks as if it was going to leave off every minute and goes on for the greater part of the afternoon.

'What sort of story?' asked Clovis, giving his croquet mallet a valedictory shove into retirement.

'One just true enough to be interesting and not true enough to be tiresome,' said the Baroness.

Clovis rearranged several cushions to his personal solace and satisfaction; he knew that the Baroness liked her guests to be comfortable, and he thought it right to respect her wishes in that particular.

'Have I ever told you the story of Saint Vespaluus?' he asked.

'You've told me stories about grand-dukes and lion-tamers and financiers' widows and a postmaster in Herzegovina,' said the Baroness, 'and about an Italian jockey and an amateur governess who went to Warsaw, and several about your mother, but certainly never anything about a saint.'

'This story happened a long while ago,' he said, 'in those uncomfortable piebald times when a third of the people were Pagan, and a third Christian, and the biggest third of all just followed whichever religion the Court happened to profess. There was a certain king called Hkrikos, who had a fearful temper and no immediate successor in his own family; his married sister, however, had provided him with a large stock of nephews from which to select his heir. And the most eligible and royally-approved of all these nephews was the sixteen-year-old Vespaluus. He was the best looking, and the best horseman and javelin-thrower, and had that priceless princely gift of being able to walk past a supplicant with an air of not having seen him, but would certainly have given something if he had.   My mother has that gift to a certain extent; she can go smilingly and financially unscathed through a charity bazaar, and meet the organizers next day with a solicitous " had I but known you were in need of funds " air that is really rather a triumph in audacity.   Now Hkrikos was a Pagan of the first water, and kept the worship of the sacred serpents, who lived in a hallowed grove on a hill near the royal palace, up to a high pitch of enthusiasm.   The common people were allowed to please themselves, within certain discreet limits, in the matter of private religion, but any official in the service of the Court who went over to the new cult was looked down on, literally as well as metaphorically, the looking down being done from the gallery that ran round the royal bear-pit.   Consequently there was considerable scandal and consternation when the youthful Vespaluus appeared one day at a Court function with a rosary tucked into his belt, and announced in reply to angry questionings that he had decided to adopt Christianity, or at any rate to give it a trial.   If it had been any of the other nephews the king would possibly have ordered something drastic in the way of scourging and banishment, but in the case of the favoured Vespaluus he determined to look on the whole thing much as a modern father might regard the announced intention of his son to adopt the stage as a profession.   He sent accordingly for the Royal Librarian. The royal library in those days was not a very extensive affair, and the keeper of the king's books had a great deal of leisure on his hands.   Consequently he was in frequent demand for the settlement of other people's affairs when these strayed beyond normal limits and got temporarily unmanageable.

' " You must reason with Prince Vespaluus,' said the king, ' and impress on him the error of his ways.   We cannot have the heir to the throne setting such a dangerous example."

' " But where shall I find the necessary arguments ? " asked the Librarian.

' " I give you free leave to pick and choose your arguments

in the royal woods and coppices," said the king; "if you cannot get together some cutting observations and stinging retorts suitable to the occasion you are a person of very poor resource."

' So the Librarian went into the woods and gathered a goodly selection of highly argumentative rods and switches, and then proceeded to reason with Vespaluus on the folly and iniquity and above all the unseemliness of his conduct.   His reasoning left a deep impression on the young prince, an impression which lasted for many weeks, during which time nothing more was heard about the unfortunate lapse into Christianity.   Then a further scandal of the same nature agitated the Court.   At a time when he should have been engaged in audibly invoking the gracious protection and patronage of the holy serpents, Vespaluus was heard singing a chant in honour of St. Odilo of Cluny.   The king was furious at this new outbreak, and began to take a gloomy view of the situation; Vespaluus was evidently going to show a dangerous obstinacy in persisting in his heresy. And yet there was nothing in his appearance to justify such perverseness; he had not the pale eye of the fanatic or the mystic look of the dreamer.   On the contrary, he was quite the best-looking boy at Court; he had an elegant, well-knit figure, a healthy complexion, eyes the colour of very ripe mulberries, and dark hair, smooth and very well cared for.'

' It sounds like a description of what you imagine yourself to have been like at the age of sixteen,' said the Baroness.

' My mother has probably been showing you some of my early photographs,' said Clovis.   Having turned the sarcasm into a compliment, he resumed his story.

' The king had Vespaluus shut up in a dark tower for three days, with nothing but bread and water to live on, the squealing and fluttering of bats to listen to, and drifting clouds to watch through one little window slit.   The anti-Pagan section of the community began to talk portentously of the boy-martyr. The martyrdom was mitigated, as far as the food was con- cerned, by the carelessness of the tower warden, who once or twice left a portion of his own supper of broiled meat and fruit and wine by mistake in the prince's cell.   After the punishment was over, Vespaluus was closely watched for any further symptom of religious perversity, for the king was determined to stand no more opposition on so important a matter, even from a favourite nephew.   If there was any more of this nonsense, he said, the succession to the throne would have to be altered.

'For a time all went well; the festival of summer sports was approaching, and the young Vespaluus was too engrossed in wrestling and foot-running and javelin-throwing competitions to bother himself with the strife of conflicting religious systems. Then, however, came the great culminating feature of the summer festival, the ceremonial dance round the grove of the sacred serpents, and Vespaluus, as we should say, "sat it out." The affront to the State religion was too public and ostentatious to be overlooked, even if the king had been so minded, and he was not in the least so minded.   For a day and a half he sat apart and brooded, and every one thought he was debating within himself the question of the young prince's death or pardon; as a matter of fact he was merely thinking out the manner of the boy's death.   As the thing had to be done, and was bound to attract an enormous amount of public attention in any case, it was as well to make it as spectacular and impressive as possible.

'"Apart from his unfortunate taste in religions," said the king, "and his obstinacy in adhering to it, he is a sweet and pleasant youth, therefore it is meet and fitting that he should be done to death by the winged envoys of sweetness."

'"Your Majesty means——?" said the Royal Librarian.

'"I mean," said the king, "that he shall be stung to death by bees.   By the royal bees, of course."

'"A most elegant death," said the Librarian.

'"Elegant and spectacular, and decidedly painful," said the king; "it fulfills all the conditions that could be wished for."

'The king himself thought out all the details of the execution ceremony. Vespaluus was to be stripped of his clothes, his hands were to be bound behind him, and he was then to be slung in a recumbent position immediately above three of the largest of the royal beehives, so that the least movement of his body would bring him in jarring contact with them. The rest could be safely left to the bees. The death throes, the king computed, might last anything from fifteen to forty minutes, though there was division of opinion and considerable wagering among the other nephews as to whether death might not be almost instantaneous, or, on the other hand, whether it might not be deferred for a couple of hours. Anyway, they all agreed, it was vastly preferable to being thrown down into an evil-smelling bear-pit and being clawed and mauled to death by imperfectly carnivorous animals.

' It so happened, however, that the keeper of the royal hives had leanings towards Christianity himself, and moreover, like most of the Court officials, he was very much attached to Vespaluus. On the eve of the execution, therefore, he busied himself with removing the stings from all the royal bees; it was a long and delicate operation, but he was an expert bee-master, and by working hard nearly all night he succeeded in disarming all, or almost all, of the hive inmates.'

' I didn't know you could take the sting from a live bee,' said the Baroness incredulously.

' Every profession has its secrets,' replied Clovis; ' if it hadn't it wouldn't be a profession. Well, the moment for the execution arrived; the king and Court took their places, and accommodation was found for as many of the populace as wished to witness the unusual spectacle. Fortunately the royal bee-yard was of considerable dimensions, and was commanded, moreover, by the terraces that ran round the royal gardens; with a little squeezing and the erection of a few platforms room was found for everybody. Vespaluus was carried into the open space in front of the hives, blushing and slightly embarrassed, but not at all displeased at the attention which was being centred on him.'

'He seems to have resembled you in more things than in appearance,' said the Baroness.

'Don't interrupt at a critical point in the story,' said Clovis.

'As soon as he had been carefully adjusted in the prescribed position over the hives, and almost before the gaolers had time to retire to a safe distance, Vespaluus gave a lusty and well-aimed kick, which sent all three hives toppling one over another. The next moment he was wrapped from head to foot in bees; each individual insect nursed the dreadful and humiliating knowledge that in this supreme hour of catastrophe it could not sting, but each felt that it ought to pretend to. Vespaluus squealed and wriggled with laughter, for he was being tickled nearly to death, and now and again he gave a furious kick and used a bad word as one of the few bees that had escaped disarmament got its protest home. But the spectators saw with amazement that he showed no signs of approaching death agony, and as the bees dropped wearily away in clusters from his body his flesh was seen to be as white and smooth as before the ordeal, with a shiny glaze from the honey-smear of innumerable bee-feet, and here and there a small red spot where one of the rare stings had left its mark. It was obvious that a miracle had been performed in his favour, and one loud murmur, of astonishment or exultation, rose from the onlooking crowd. The king gave orders for Vespaluus to be taken down to await further orders, and stalked silently back to his midday meal, at which he was careful to eat heartily and drink copiously as though nothing unusual had happened. After dinner he sent for the Royal Librarian.

' "What is the meaning of this fiasco?" he demanded.

' "Your Majesty," said that official, "either there is something radically wrong with the bees——"

' "There is nothing wrong with my bees," said the king haughtily, "they are the best bees."

' "Or else," said the Librarian, "there is something irremediably right about Prince Vespaluus."

' "If Vespaluus is right I must be wrong," said the king.

'The Librarian was silent for a moment. Hasty speech has been the downfall of many; ill-considered silence was the undoing of the luckless Court functionary.

'Forgetting the restraint due to his dignity, and the golden rule which imposes repose of mind and body after a heavy meal, the king rushed upon the keeper of the royal books and hit him repeatedly and promiscuously over the head with an ivory chessboard, a pewter wine-flagon, and a brass candlestick; he knocked him violently and often against an iron torch sconce, and kicked him thrice round the banqueting chamber with rapid, energetic kicks. Finally, he dragged him down a long passage by the hair of his head and flung him out of a window into the courtyard below.'

'Was he much hurt?' asked the Baroness.

'More hurt than surprised,' said Clovis. 'You see, the king was notorious for his violent temper. However, this was the first time he had let himself go so unrestrainedly on the top of a heavy meal. The Librarian lingered for many days—in fact, for all I know, he may have ultimately recovered, but Hkrikros died that same evening. Vespaluus had hardly finished getting the honey stains off his body before a hurried deputation came to put the coronation oil on his head. And what with the publicly-witnessed miracle and the accession of a Christian sovereign, it was not surprising that there was a general scramble of converts to the new religion. A hastily consecrated bishop was overworked with a rush of baptisms in the hastily improvised Cathedral of St. Odilo. And the boy-martyr-that-might-have-been was transposed in the popular imagination into a royal boy-saint, whose fame attracted throngs of curious and devout sightseers to the capital. Vespaluus, who was busily engaged in organizing the games and athletic contests that were to mark the commencement of his reign, had no time to give heed to the religious fervour which was effervescing round his personality; the first indication he had of the existing state of affairs was when the Court Chamberlain (a recent and very ardent addition to the Christian community) brought for his approval the outlines of a projected ceremonial cutting-down of the idolatrous serpent-grove.

' " Your Majesty will be graciously pleased to cut down the first tree with a specially consecrated axe," said the obsequious official.

' " I'll cut off your head first, with any axe that comes handy," said Vespaluus indignantly; " do you suppose that I'm going to begin my reign by mortally affronting the sacred serpents? It would be most unlucky."

' " But your Majesty's Christian principles? " exclaimed the bewildered Chamberlain.

' " I never had any," said Vespaluus; " I used to pretend to be a Christian convert just to annoy Hkrikros. He used to fly into such delicious tempers. And it was rather fun being whipped and scolded and shut up in a tower all for nothing. But as to turning Christian in real earnest, like you people seem to do, I couldn't think of such a thing. And the holy and esteemed serpents have always helped me when I've prayed to them for success in my running and wrestling and hunting, and it was through their distinguished intercession that the bees were not able to hurt me with their stings. It would be black ingratitude to turn against their worship at the very outset of my reign. I hate you for suggesting it."

' The Chamberlain wrung his hands despairingly.

' " But, your Majesty," he wailed, " the people are reverencing you as a saint, and the nobles are being Christianized in batches, and neighbouring potentates of that Faith are sending special envoys to welcome you as a brother. There is some talk of making you the patron saint of beehives, and a certain shade of honey-yellow has been christened Vespaluusian gold at the Emperor's Court. You can't surely go back on all this."

' " I don't mind being reverenced and greeted and honoured," said Vespaluus; " I don't even mind being sainted in moderation, as long as I'm not expected to be saintly as well. But I wish you clearly and finally to understand that I will *not* give up the worship of the august and auspicious serpents."

' There was a world of unspoken bear-pit in the way he uttered those last words, and the mulberry-dark eyes flashed dangerously.

' " A new reign," said the Chamberlain to himself, " but the same old temper."

' Finally, as a State necessity, the matter of the religions was compromised. At stated intervals the king appeared before his subjects in the national cathedral in the character of St. Vespaluus, and the idolatrous grove was gradually pruned and lopped away till nothing remained of it. But the sacred and esteemed serpents were removed to a private shrubbery in the royal gardens, where Vespaluus the Pagan and certain members of his household devoutly and decently worshipped them. That possibly is the reason why the boy-king's success in sports and hunting never deserted him to the end of his days, and that is also the reason why, in spite of the popular veneration for his sanctity, he never received official canonization.'

' It has stopped raining,' said the Baroness.

THE WAY TO THE DAIRY

The Baroness and Clovis sat in a much-frequented corner of the Park exchanging biographical confidences about the long succession of passers-by.

' Who are those depressed-looking young women who have just gone by? ' asked the Baroness; ' they have the air of people who have bowed to destiny and are not quite sure whether the salute will be returned.'

' Those,' said Clovis, ' are the Brimley Bomefields. I dare say you would look depressed if you had been through their experiences.'

' I'm always having depressing experiences,' said the Baroness, ' but I never give them outward expression. It's as bad as looking one's age. Tell me about the Brimley Bomefields.'

' Well,' said Clovis, ' the beginning of their tragedy was that they found an aunt. The aunt had been there all the time, but they had very nearly forgotten her existence until a distant relative refreshed their memory by remembering her very distinctly in his will; it is wonderful what the force of example will accomplish. The aunt, who had been unobtrusively poor, became quite pleasantly rich, and the Brimley Bomefields grew suddenly concerned at the loneliness of her life and took her under their collective wings. She had as many wings around her at this time as one of those beast-things in Revelation.'

' So far I don't see any tragedy from the Brimley Bomefields' point of view,' said the Baroness.

' We haven't got to it yet,' said Clovis. ' The aunt had been used to living very simply, and had seen next to nothing of what we should consider life, and her nieces didn't encourage her to do much in the way of making a splash with her money. Quite a good deal of it would come to them at her death, and she was a fairly old woman, but there was one circumstance which cast a shadow of gloom over the satisfaction they felt in the discovery and acquisition of this desirable aunt: she openly acknowledged that a comfortable slice of her little fortune would go to a nephew on the other side of her family. He was rather a deplorable thing in rotters, and quite hopelessly top-hole in the way of getting through money, but he had been more or less decent to the old lady in her unremembered days, and she wouldn't hear anything against him. At least, she wouldn't pay any attention to what she did hear, but her nieces took care that she should have to listen to a good deal in that line. It seemed such a pity, they said among themselves, that good money should fall into such worthless hands. They habitually spoke of their aunt's money as " good money," as though other people's aunts dabbled for the most part in spurious currency.

' Regularly after the Derby, St. Leger, and other notable racing events they indulged in audible speculations as to how much money Roger had squandered in unfortunate betting transactions.

' " His travelling expenses must come to a big sum," said the eldest Brimley Bomefield one day; " they say he attends every race-meeting in England, besides others abroad. I shouldn't wonder if he went all the way to India to see the race for the Calcutta Sweepstake that one hears so much about."

' " Travel enlarges the mind, my dear Christine," said her aunt.

' " Yes, dear aunt, travel undertaken in the right spirit," agreed Christine; " but travel pursued merely as a means towards gambling and extravagant living is more likely to contract the purse than to enlarge the mind. However, as long as Roger enjoys himself, I suppose he doesn't care how fast or unprofitably the money goes, or where he is to find more. It seems a pity, that's all."

' The aunt by that time had begun to talk of something else, and it was doubtful if Christine's moralizing had been even accorded a hearing. It was her remark, however—the aunt's remark, I mean—about travel enlarging the mind, that gave the youngest Brimley Bomefield her great idea for the showing-up of Roger.

' " If aunt could only be taken somewhere to see him gambling and throwing away money," she said, " it would open her eyes to his character more effectually than anything we can say."

' " My dear Veronique," said her sisters, " we can't go following him to race-meetings."

' " Certainly not to race-meetings," said Veronique, " but we might go to some place where one can look on at gambling without taking part in it."

' " Do you mean Monte Carlo ? " they asked her, beginning to jump rather at the idea.

' " Monte Carlo is a long way off, and has a dreadful reputation," said Veronique; " I shouldn't like to tell our friends that we were going to Monte Carlo. But I believe Roger usually goes to Dieppe about this time of year, and some quite respectable English people go there, and the journey wouldn't be expensive. If aunt could stand the Channel crossing the change of scene might do her a lot of good."

' And that was how the fateful idea came to the Brimley Bomefields.

' From the very first set-off disaster hung over the expedition, as they afterwards remembered. To begin with, all the Brimley Bomefields were extremely unwell during the crossing, while the aunt enjoyed the sea air and made friends with all manner of strange travelling companions. Then, although it was many years since she had been on the Continent, she had served a very practical apprenticeship there as a paid companion, and her knowledge of colloquial French beat theirs to a standstill. It became increasingly difficult to keep under their collective wings a person who knew what she wanted and was able to ask for it and to see that she got it. Also, as far as Roger was concerned, they drew Dieppe blank; it turned out that he was staying at Pourville, a little watering-place a mile or two further west. The Brimley Bomefields discovered that Dieppe was too crowded and frivolous, and persuaded the old lady to migrate to the comparative seclusion of Pourville.

' " You won't find it dull, you know," they assured her; " there is a little casino attached to the hotel, and you can watch the people dancing and throwing away their money at *petits chevaux.*"

' It was just before *petits chevaux* had been supplanted by *boule.*

' Roger was not staying in the same hotel, but they knew that the casino would be certain of his patronage on most afternoons and evenings.

' On the first evening of their visit they wandered into the casino after a fairly early dinner, and hovered near the tables. Bertie van Tahn was staying there at the time, and he described the whole incident to me. The Brimley Bomefields kept a furtive watch on the doors as though they were expecting some one to turn up, and the aunt got more and more amused and interested watching the little horses whirl round and round the board.

' " Do you know, poor little number eight hasn't won for the last thirty-two times,' she said to Christine; " I've been keeping count. I shall really have to put five francs on him to encourage him."

' " Come and watch the dancing, dear," said Christine nervously. It was scarcely a part of their strategy that Roger should come in and find the old lady backing her fancy at the *petits chevaux* table.

' " Just wait while I put five francs on number eight," said the aunt, and in another moment her money was lying on the table. The horses commenced to move round; it was a slow race this time, and number eight crept up at the finish like some crafty demon and placed his nose just a fraction in front of number three, who had seemed to be winning easily. Recourse had to be had to measurement, and the number eight was proclaimed the winner. The aunt picked up thirty-five francs. After that the Brimley Bomefields would have had to have used concerted force to get her away from the tables. When Roger appeared on the scene she was fifty-two francs to the good; her nieces were hovering forlornly in the background, like chickens that have been hatched out by a duck and are despairingly watching their parent disporting herself in a dangerous and uncongenial element. The supper-party which Roger insisted on standing that night in honour of his aunt and the three Miss Brimley Bomefields was remarkable for the unrestrained gaiety of two of the participants and the funereal mirthlessness of the remaining guests.

'"I do not think," Christine confided afterwards to a friend, who re-confided it to Bertie van Tahn, "that I shall ever be able to touch *pâté de foie gras* again. It would bring back memories of that awful evening."

'For the next two or three days the nieces made plans for returning to England or moving on to some other resort where there was no casino. The aunt was busy making a system for winning at *petits chevaux*. Number eight, her first love, had been running rather unkindly for her, and a series of plunges on number five had turned out even worse.

'"Do you know, I dropped over seven hundred francs at the tables this afternoon," she announced cheerfully at dinner on the fourth evening of their visit.

'"Aunt! Twenty-eight pounds! And you were losing last night too."

'"Oh, I shall get it all back," she said optimistically; "but not here. These silly little horses are no good. I shall go somewhere where one can play comfortably at roulette. You needn't look so shocked. I've always felt that, given the opportunity, I should be an inveterate gambler, and now you darlings have put the opportunity in my way. I must drink your very good healths. Waiter, a bottle of *Pontet Canet*. Ah, it's number seven on the wine list; I shall plunge on number seven to-night. It won four times running this afternoon when I was backing that silly number five."

'Number seven was not in a winning mood that evening.

The Brimley Bomefields, tired of watching disaster from a distance, drew near to the table where their aunt was now an honoured habituée, and gazed mournfully at the successive victories of one and five and eight and four, which swept " good money " out of the purse of seven's obstinate backer. The day's losses totalled something very near two thousand francs.

' " You incorrigible gamblers," said Roger chaffingly to them when he found them at the tables.

' " We are not gambling," said Christine freezingly; " we are looking on."

' " I *don't* think," said Roger knowingly; " of course you're a syndicate and aunt is putting the stakes on for all of you. Anyone can tell by your looks when the wrong horse wins that you've got a stake on."

' Aunt and nephew had supper alone that night, or at least they would have if Bertie hadn't joined them; all the Brimley Bomefields had headaches.

' The aunt carried them all off to Dieppe the next day and set cheerily about the task of winning back some of her losses. Her luck was variable; in fact, she had some fair streaks of good fortune, just enough to keep her thoroughly amused with her new distraction; but on the whole she was a loser. The Brimley Bomefields had a collective attack of nervous prostration on the day when she sold out a quantity of shares in Argentine rails. " Nothing will ever bring that money back," they remarked lugubriously to one another.

' Veronique at last could bear it no longer, and went home; you see, it had been her idea to bring the aunt on this disastrous expedition, and though the others did not cast the fact verbally in her face, there was a certain lurking reproach in their eyes which was harder to meet than actual upbraidings. The other two remained behind, forlornly mounting guard over their aunt until such time as the waning of the Dieppe season should at last turn her in the direction of home and safety. They made anxious calculations as to how little " good money " might, with reasonable luck, be squandered in the meantime.   Here, however, their reckoning went far astray; the close of the Dieppe season merely turned their aunt's thoughts in search of some other convenient gambling resort.   " Show a cat the way to the dairy——" I forget how the proverb goes on, but it summed up the situation as far as the Brimley Bome-fields' aunt was concerned.   She had been introduced to un-explored pleasures, and found them greatly to her liking, and she was in no hurry to forgo the fruits of her newly acquired knowledge.   You see, for the first time in her life the old thing was thoroughly enjoying herself; she was losing money, but she had plenty of fun and excitement over the process, and she had enough left to do very comfortably on.   Indeed, she was only just learning to understand the art of doing oneself well. She was a popular hostess, and in return her fellow-gamblers were always ready to entertain her to dinners and suppers when their luck was in.   Her nieces, who still remained in attendance on her, with the pathetic unwillingness of a crew to leave a foundering treasure ship which might yet be steered into port, found little pleasure in these Bohemian festivities; to see " good money " lavished on good living for the entertainment of a nondescript circle of acquaintances who were not likely to be in any way socially useful to them, did not attune them to a spirit of revelry.   They contrived, whenever possible, to excuse themselves from participation in their aunt's deplored gaieties; the Brimley Bomefield headaches became famous.

' And one day the nieces came to the conclusion that, as they would have expressed it, " no useful purpose would be served " by their continued attendance on a relative who had so thoroughly emancipated herself from the sheltering protection of their wings.   The aunt bore the announcement of their departure with a cheerfulness that was almost disconcerting.

' " It's time you went home and had those headaches seen to by a specialist," was her comment on the situation.

' The homeward journey of the Brimley Bomefields was a veritable retreat from Moscow, and what made it the more bitter was the fact that the Moscow, in this case, was not over-whelmed with fire and ashes, but merely extravagantly over-illuminated.

'From mutual friends and acquaintances they sometimes get glimpses of their prodigal relative, who has settled down into a confirmed gambling maniac, living on such salvage of income as obliging moneylenders have left at her disposal.

'So you need not be surprised,' concluded Clovis, 'if they do wear a depressed look in public.'

'Which is Veronique?' asked the Baroness.

'The most depressed-looking of the three,' said Clovis.

THE PEACE OFFERING

' I WANT you to help me in getting up a dramatic entertainment
of some sort,' said the Baroness to Clovis. ' You see, there's
been an election petition down here, and a member unseated
and no end of bitterness and ill-feeling, and the County is
socially divided against itself. I thought a play of some kind
would be an excellent opportunity for bringing people together
again, and giving them something to think of besides tiresome
political squabbles.'

The Baroness was evidently ambitious of reproducing
beneath her own roof the pacifying effects traditionally ascribed
to the celebrated Reel of Tullochgorum.

' We might do something on the lines of Greek tragedy,'
said Clovis, after due reflection; ' the Return of Agamemnon,
for instance.'

The Baroness frowned.

' It sounds rather reminiscent of an election result, doesn't
it?'

' It wasn't that sort of return,' explained Clovis; ' it was a
home-coming.'

' I thought you said it was a tragedy.'

' Well, it was. He was killed in his bathroom, you know.'

' Oh, now I know the story, of course. Do you want me to
take the part of Charlotte Corday?'

' That's a different story and a different century,' said Clovis;
' the dramatic unities forbid one to lay a scene in more than one
century at a time. The killing in this case has to be done by
Clytemnestra.'

' Rather a pretty name. I'll do that part. I suppose you
want to be Aga—whatever his name is?'

' Dear no. Agamemnon was the father of grown-up children, and probably wore a beard and looked prematurely aged.
I shall be his charioteer or bath-attendant, or something decora-

tive of that kind. We must do everything in the Sumurun manner, you know.'

'I don't know,' said the Baroness; 'at least, I should know better if you would explain exactly what you mean by the Sumurun manner.'

Clovis obliged: 'Weird music, and exotic skippings and flying leaps, and lots of drapery and undrapery. Particularly undrapery."

'I think I told you the County are coming. The County won't stand anything very Greek.'

'You can get over any objection by calling it Hygiene, or limb-culture, or something of that sort. After all, every one exposes their insides to the public gaze and sympathy nowadays, so why not one's outside?'

'My dear boy, I can ask the County to a Greek play, or to a costume play, but to a Greek-costume play, never. It doesn't do to let the dramatic instinct carry one too far; one must consider one's environment. When one lives among greyhounds one should avoid giving life-like imitations of a rabbit, unless one want's one's head snapped off. Remember, I've got this place on a seven years' lease. And then,' continued the Baroness, 'as to skippings and flying leaps; I must ask Emily Dushford to take a part. She's a dear good thing, and will do anything she's told, or try to; but can you imagine her doing a flying leap under any circumstances?'

'She can be Cassandra, and she need only take flying leaps into the future, in a metaphorical sense.'

'Cassandra; rather a pretty name. What kind of character is she?"

'She was a sort of advance-agent for calamities. To know her was to know the worst. Fortunately for the gaiety of the age she lived in, no one took her very seriously. Still, it must have been fairly galling to have her turning up after every catastrophe with a conscious air of " perhaps another time you'll believe what I say."'

'I should have wanted to kill her.'

'As Clytemnestra I believe you gratify that very natural wish.'

'Then it has a happy ending, in spite of it being a tragedy?'

'Well, hardly,' said Clovis; 'you see, the satisfaction of putting a violent end to Cassandra must have been considerably damped by the fact that she had foretold what was going to happen to her. She probably dies with an intensely irritating "what-did-I-tell-you" smile on her lips. By the way, of course all the killing will be done in the Sumurun manner.'

'Please explain again,' said the Baroness, taking out a note-book and pencil.

'Little and often, you know, instead of one sweeping blow. You see, you are at your own home, so there's no need to hurry over the murdering as though it were some disagreeable but necessary duty.'

'And what sort of end do I have? I mean, what curtain do I get?'

'I suppose you rush into your lover's arms. That is where one of the flying leaps will come in.'

The getting-up and rehearsing of the play seemed likely to cause, in a restricted area, nearly as much heart-burning and ill-feeling as the election petition. Clovis, as adapter and stage-manager, insisted, as far as he was able, on the charioteer being quite the most prominent character in the play, and his panther-skin tunic caused almost as much trouble and discussion as Clytemnestra's spasmodic succession of lovers, who broke down on probation with alarming uniformity. When the cast was at length fixed beyond hope of reprieve matters went scarcely more smoothly. Clovis and the Baroness rather overdid the Sumurun manner, while the rest of the company could hardly be said to attempt it at all. As for Cassandra, who was expected to improvise her own prophecies, she appeared to be as incapable of taking flying leaps into futurity as of executing more than a severely plantigrade walk across the stage.

'Woe! Trojans, woe to Troy!' was the most inspired

remark she could produce after several hours of conscientious study of all the available authorities.

'It's no earthly use foretelling the fall of Troy,' expostulated Clovis, 'because Troy has fallen before the action of the play begins. And you mustn't say too much about your own impending doom either, because that will give things away too much to the audience.'

After several minutes of painful brain-searching, Cassandra smiled reassuringly.

'I know. I'll predict a long and happy reign for George the Fifth.'

'My dear girl,' protested Clovis, 'have you reflected that Cassandra specialized in foretelling calamities?'

There was another prolonged pause and another triumphant issue.

'I know. I'll foretell a most disastrous season for the foxhounds.'

'On no account,' entreated Clovis; 'do remember that all Cassandra's predictions came true. The M.F.H. and the Hunt Secretary are both awfully superstititous, and they are both going to be present.'

Cassandra retreated hastily to her bedroom to bathe her eyes before appearing at tea.

The Baroness and Clovis were by this time scarcely on speaking terms. Each sincerely wished their respective rôle to be the pivot round which the entire production should revolve, and each lost no opportunity for furthering the cause they had at heart. As fast as Clovis introduced some effective bit of business for the charioteer (and he introduced a great many), the Baroness would remorselessly cut it out, or more often dovetail it into her own part, while Clovis retaliated in a similar fashion whenever possible. The climax came when Clytemnestra annexed some highly complimentary lines, which were to have been addressed to the charioteer by a bevy of admiring Greek damsels, and put them into the mouth of her lover. Clovis stood by in apparent unconcern while the words:

' Oh, lovely stripling, radiant as the dawn,' were transposed into:

' Oh, Clytemnestra, radiant as the dawn,' but there was a dangerous glitter in his eye that might have given the Baroness warning. He had composed the verse himself, inspired and thoroughly carried away by his subject; he suffered, therefore, a double pang in beholding his tribute deflected from its destined object, and his words mutilated and twisted into what became an extravagant panegyric on the Baroness's personal charms. It was from this moment that he became gentle and assiduous in his private coaching of Cassandra.

The County, forgetting its dissensions, mustered in full strength to witness the much-talked-of production. The protective Providence that looks after little children and amateur theatricals made good its traditional promise that everything should be right on the night. The Baroness and Clovis seemed to have sunk their mutual differences, and between them dominated the scene to the partial eclipse of all the other characters, who, for the most part, seemed well content to remain in the shadow. Even Agamemnon, with ten years of strenuous life around Troy standing to his credit, appeared to be an unobtrusive personality compared with his flamboyant charioteer. But the moment came for Cassandra (who had been excused from any very definite outpourings during rehearsals) to support her rôle by delivering herself of a few well-chosen anticipations of pending misfortune. The musicians obliged with appropriately lugubrious wailings and thumpings, and the Baroness seized the opportunity to make a dash to the dressing-room to effect certain repairs in her make-up. Cassandra, nervous but resolute, came down to the footlights and, like one repeating a carefully learned lesson, flung her remarks straight at the audience:

' I see woe for this fair country if the brood of corrupt, self-seeking, unscrupulous, unprincipled politicians ' (here she named one of the two rival parties in the State) ' continue to infest and poison our local councils and undermine our Parliamentary representation; if they continue to snatch votes by nefarious and discreditable means——'

A humming as of a great hive of bewildered and affronted bees drowned her further remarks and wore down the droning of the musicians.   The Baroness, who should have been greeted on her return to the stage with the pleasing invocation, ' Oh, Clytemnestra, radiant as the dawn,' heard instead the imperious voice of Lady Thistledale ordering her carriage, and something like a storm of open discord going on at the back of the room.

.   .   .

The social divisions in the County healed themselves after their own fashion; both parties found common ground in condemning the Baroness's outrageously bad taste and tact-lessness.

She has been fortunate in sub-letting for the greater part of her seven years' lease.

THE PEACE OF MOWSLE BARTON

CREFTON LOCKYER sat at his ease, an ease alike of body and soul, in the little patch of ground, half-orchard and half-garden, that abutted on the farmyard at Mowsle Barton. After the stress and noise of long years of city life, the repose and peace of the hill-begirt homestead struck on his senses with an almost dramatic intensity. Time and space seemed to lose their meaning and their abruptness; the minutes slid away into hours, and the meadows and fallows sloped away into middle distance, softly and imperceptibly. Wild weeds of the hedge-row straggled into the flower-garden, and wallflowers and garden bushes made counter-raids into farmyard and lane. Sleepy-looking hens and solemn preoccupied ducks were equally at home in yard, orchard, or roadway; nothing seemed to belong definitely to anywhere; even the gates were not necessarily to be found on their hinges. And over the whole scene brooded the sense of a peace that had almost a quality of magic in it. In the afternoon you felt that it had always been afternoon, and must always remain afternoon; in the twilight you knew that it could never have been anything else but twilight. Crefton Lockyer sat at his ease in the rustic seat beneath an old medlar tree, and decided that here was the life-anchorage that his mind had so fondly pictured and that latterly his tired and jarred senses had so often pined for. He would make a permanent lodging-place among these simple friendly people, gradually increasing the modest comforts with which he would like to surround himself, but falling in as much as possible with their manner of living.

As he slowly matured this resolution in his mind an elderly woman came hobbling with uncertain gait through the orchard. He recognized her as a member of the farm household, the mother or possibly the mother-in-law of Mrs. Spurfield, his present landlady, and hastily formulated some pleasant remark to make to her. She forestalled him.

" There's a bit of writing chalked up on the door over yonder. What is it? "

She spoke in a dull impersonal manner, as though the question had been on her lips for years and had best be got rid of. Her eyes, however, looked impatiently over Crefton's head at the door of a small barn which formed the outpost of a straggling line of farm buildings.

" Martha Pillamon is an old witch " was the announcement that met Crefton's inquiring scrutiny, and he hesitated a moment before giving the statement wider publicity. For all he knew to the contrary, it might be Martha herself to whom he was speaking. It was possible that Mrs. Spurfield's maiden name had been Pillamon. And the gaunt, withered old dame at his side might certainly fulfil local conditions as to the outward aspect of a witch.

' It's something about some one called Martha Pillamon,' he explained cautiously.

' What does it say? '

' It's very disrespectful,' said Crefton; ' it says she's a witch. Such things ought not to be written up.'

' It's true, every word of it,' said his listener with considerable satisfaction, adding as a special descriptive note of her own, ' the old toad.'

And as she hobbled away through the farmyard she shrilled out in her cracked voice, ' Martha Pillamon is an old witch! '

' Did you hear what she said? ' mumbled a weak, angry voice somewhere behind Crefton's shoulder. Turning hastily, he beheld another old crone, thin and yellow and wrinkled, and evidently in a high state of displeasure. Obviously this was Martha Pillamon in person. The orchard seemed to be a favourite promenade for the aged women of the neighbourhood.

' 'Tis lies, 'tis sinful lies,' the weak voice went on. ' 'Tis Betsy Croot is the old witch. She an' her daughter, the dirty rat. I'll put a spell on 'em, the old nuisances.'

As she limped slowly away her eye caught the chalk inscription on the barn door.

'What's written up there?' she demanded, wheeling round on Crefton.

'Vote for Soarker,' he responded, with the craven boldness of the practised peacemaker.

The old woman grunted, and her mutterings and her faded red shawl lost themselves gradually among the tree-trunks. Crefton rose presently and made his way towards the farm-house. Somehow a good deal of the peace seemed to have slipped out of the atmosphere.

The cheery bustle of tea-time in the old farm kitchen, which Crefton had found so agreeable on previous afternoons, seemed to have soured to-day into a certain uneasy melancholy. There was a dull, dragging silence around the board, and the tea itself, when Crefton came to taste it, was a flat, lukewarm concoction that would have driven the spirit of revelry out of a carnival.

'It's no use complaining of the tea,' said Mrs. Spurfield hastily, as her guest stared with an air of polite inquiry at his cup. 'The kettle won't boil, that's the truth of it.'

Crefton turned to the hearth, where an unusually fierce fire was banked up under a big black kettle, which sent a thin wreath of steam from its spout, but seemed otherwise to ignore the action of the roaring blaze beneath it.

'It's been there more than an hour, an' boil it won't,' said Mrs. Spurfield, adding, by way of complete explanation, 'we're bewitched.'

'It's Martha Pillamon as has done it,' chimed in the old mother; 'I'll be even with the old toad. I'll put a spell on her.'

'It must boil in time,' protested Crefton, ignoring the suggestions of foul influences. 'Perhaps the coal is damp.'

'It won't boil in time for supper, nor for breakfast to-morrow morning, not if you was to keep the fire a-going all night for it," said Mrs. Spurfield. And it didn't. The household

subsisted on fried and baked dishes, and a neighbour obligingly
brewed tea and sent it across in a moderately warm condition.

'I suppose you'll be leaving us, now that things has turned
up uncomfortable,' Mrs. Spurfield observed at breakfast;
'there are folks as deserts one as soon as trouble comes.'

Crefton hurriedly disclaimed any immediate change of plans;
he observed, however, to himself that the earlier heartiness of
manner had in a large measure deserted the household.   Sus-
picious looks, sulky silences, or sharp speeches had become the
order of the day.   As for the old mother, she sat about the
kitchen or the garden all day, murmuring threats and spells
against Martha Pillamon.   There was something alike terrifying and piteous in the spectacle of these frail old morsels of
humanity consecrating their last flickering energies to the
task of making each other wretched.   Hatred seemed to be the
one faculty which had survived in undiminished vigour and
intensity where all else was dropping into ordered and sym-
metrical decay.   And the uncanny part of it was that some
horrid unwholesome power seemed to be distilled from their
spite and their cursings.   No amount of sceptical explanation
could remove the undoubted fact that neither kettle nor sauce-
pan would come to boiling-point over the hottest fire.   Crefton
clung as long as possible to the theory of some defect in the
coals, but a wood fire gave the same result, and when a small
spirit-lamp kettle, which he ordered out by carrier, showed the
same obstinate refusal to allow its contents to boil he felt that
he had come suddenly into contact with some unguessed-
at and very evil aspect of hidden forces.   Miles away, down
through an opening in the hills, he could catch glimpses of a road
where motor-cars sometimes passed, and yet here, so little removed from the arteries of the latest civilization, was a bat-
haunted old homestead, where something unmistakably like
witchcraft seemed to hold a very practical sway.

Passing out through the farm garden on his way to the lanes
beyond, where he hoped to recapture the comfortable sense of
peacefulness that was so lacking around house and hearth—

especially hearth—Crefton came across the old mother, sitting mumbling to herself in the seat beneath the medlar tree. ' Let un sink as swims, let un sink as swims,' she was repeating over and over again, as a child repeats a half-learned lesson. And 'now and then she would break off into a shrill laugh, with a note of malice in it that was not pleasant to hear. Crefton was glad when he found himself out of earshot, in the quiet and seclusion of the deep overgrown lanes that seemed to lead away to nowhere; one, narrower and deeper than the rest, attracted his footsteps, and he was almost annoyed when he found that it really did act as a miniature roadway to a human dwelling. A forlorn-looking cottage with a scrap of ill-tended cabbage garden and a few aged apple trees stood at an angle where a swift-flowing stream widened out for a space into a decent-sized pond before hurrying away again through the willows that had checked its course. Crefton leaned against a tree-trunk and looked across the swirling eddies of the pond at the humble little homestead opposite him; the only sign of life came from a small procession of dingy-looking ducks that marched in single file down to the water's edge. There is always something rather taking in the way a duck changes itself in an instant from a slow, clumsy waddler of the earth to a graceful, buoyant swimmer of the waters, and Crefton waited with a certain arrested attention to watch the leader of the file launch itself on to the surface of the pond. He was aware at the same time of a curious warning instinct that something strange and unpleasant was about to happen. The duck flung itself confidently forward into the water, and rolled immediately under the surface. Its head appeared for a moment and went under again, leaving a train of bubbles in its wake, while wings and legs churned the water in an helpless swirl of flapping and kicking. The bird was obviously drowning. Crefton thought at first that it had caught itself in some weeds, or was being attacked from below by a pike or water-rat. But no blood floated to the surface, and the wildly bobbing body made the circuit of the pond current without hindrance from any entanglement. A second duck had by this time launched itself into the pond, and a second struggling body rolled and twisted under the surface. There was something peculiarly piteous in the sight of the gasping beaks that showed now and again above the water, as though in terrified protest at this treachery of a trusted and familiar element. Crefton gazed with something like horror as a third duck poised itself on the bank and splashed in, to share the fate of the other two. He felt almost relieved when the remainder of the flock, taking tardy alarm from the commotion of the slowly drowning bodies, drew themselves up with tense outstretched necks, and sidled away from the scene of danger, quacking a deep note of disquietude as they went. At the same moment Crefton became aware that he was not the only human witness of the scene; a bent and withered old woman, whom he recognized at once as Martha Pillamon, of sinister reputation, had limped down the cottage path to the water's edge, and was gazing fixedly at the gruesome whirligig of dying birds that went in horrible procession round the pool. Presently her voice rang out in a shrill note of quavering rage:

'' 'Tis Betsy Croot adone it, the old rat. I'll put a spell on her, see if I don't.'

Crefton slipped quietly away, uncertain whether or no the old woman had noticed his presence. Even before she had proclaimed the guiltiness of Betsy Croot, the latter's muttered incantation ' Let un sink as swims ' had flashed uncomfortably across his mind. But it was the final threat of a retaliatory spell which crowded his mind with misgiving to the exclusion of all other thoughts or fancies. His reasoning powers could no longer afford to dismiss these old-wives' threats as empty bickerings. The household at Mowsle Barton lay under the displeasure of a vindictive old woman who seemed able to materialize her personal spites in a very practical fashion, and there was no saying what form her revenge for three drowned ducks might not take. As a member of the household Crefton might find himself involved in some general and highly disagreeable visitation of Martha Pillamon's wrath. Of course he knew that he was giving way to absurd fancies, but the behaviour of the spirit-lamp kettle and the subsequent scene at the pond had considerably unnerved him. And the vagueness of his alarm added to its terrors; when once you have taken the Impossible into your calculations its possibilities become practically limitless.

Crefton rose at his usual early hour the next morning, after one of the least restful nights he had spent at the farm. His sharpened senses quickly detected that subtle atmosphere of things-being-not-altogether-well that hangs over a stricken household. The cows had been milked, but they stood huddled about in the yard, waiting impatiently to be driven out afield, and the poultry kept up an importunate querulous reminder of deferred feeding-time; the yard pump, which usually made discordant music at frequent intervals during the early morning, was to-day ominously silent. In the house itself there was a coming and going of scuttering footsteps, a rushing and dying away of hurried voices, and long, uneasy stillnesses. Crefton finished his dressing and made his way to the head of a narrow staircase. He could hear a dull, complaining voice, a voice into which an awed hush had crept, and recognized the speaker as Mrs. Spurfield.

'He'll go away, for sure,' the voice was saying; 'there are those as runs away from one as soon as real misfortune shows itself.'

Crefton felt that he probably was one of 'those,' and that there were moments when it was advisable to be true to type.

He crept back to his room, collected and packed his few belongings, placed the money due for his lodgings on a table, and made his way out by a back door into the yard. A mob of poultry surged expectantly towards him; shaking off their interested attentions he hurried along under cover of cowstall, piggery, and hayricks till he reached the lane at the back of the farm. A few minutes' walk, which only the burden of his portmanteaux restrained from developing into an undisguised run, brought him to a main road, where the early carrier soon overtook him and sped him onward to the neighbouring town. At a bend of the road he caught a last glimpse of the farm; the old gabled roofs and thatched barns, the straggling orchard, and the medlar tree, with its wooden seat, stood out with an almost spectral clearness in the early morning light, and over it all brooded that air of magic possession which Crefton had once mistaken for peace.

The bustle and roar of Paddington Station smote on his ears with a welcome protective greeting.

' Very bad for our nerves, all this rush and hurry,' said a fellow-traveller; ' give me the peace and quiet of the country.'

Crefton mentally surrendered his share of the desired commodity. A crowded, brilliantly over-lighted music-hall, where an exuberant rendering of ' 1812 ' was being given by a strenuous orchestra, came nearest to his ideal of a nerve sedative.

THE TALKING-OUT OF
TARRINGTON

'HEAVENS!' exclaimed the aunt of Clovis, 'here's some one I know bearing down on us. I can't remember his name, but he lunched with us once in Town. Tarrington—yes, that's it. He's heard of the picnic I'm giving for the Princess, and he'll cling to me like a lifebelt till I give him an invitation; then he'll ask if he may bring all his wives and mothers and sisters with him. That's the worst of these small watering-places; one can't escape from anybody.'

'I'll fight a rearguard action for you if you like to do a bolt now,' volunteered Clovis; 'you've a clear ten yards start if you don't lose time.'

The aunt of Clovis responded gamely to the suggestion, and churned away like a Nile steamer, with a long brown ripple of Pekingese spaniel trailing in her wake.

'Pretend you don't know him,' was her parting advice, tinged with the reckless courage of the non-combatant.

The next moment the overtures of an affably disposed gentleman were being received by Clovis with a 'silent-upon-a-peak-in-Darien' stare which denoted an absence of all previous acquaintance with the object scrutinized.

'I expect you don't know me with my moustache,' said the new-comer; 'I've only grown it during the last two months.'

'On the contrary,' said Clovis, 'the moustache is the only thing about you that seemed familiar to me. I felt certain that I had met it somewhere before.'

'My name is Tarrington,' resumed the candidate for recognition.

'A very useful kind of name,' said Clovis; 'with a name of that sort no one would blame you if you did nothing in particular heroic or remarkable, would they? And yet if you were to raise a troop of light horse in a moment of national emergency,

"Tarrington's Light Horse" would sound quite appropriate and pulse-quickening; whereas if you were called Spoopin, for instance, the thing would be out of the question. No one, even in a moment of national emergency, could possibly belong to Spoopin's Horse.'

The new-comer smiled weakly, as one who is not to be put off by mere flippancy, and began again with patient persistence:

'I think you ought to remember my name——'

'I shall,' said Clovis, with an air of immense sincerity. 'My aunt was asking me only this morning to suggest names for four young owls she's just had sent her as pets. I shall call them all Tarrington; then if one or two of them die or fly away, or leave us in any of the ways that pet owls are prone to, there will be always one or two left to carry on your name. And my aunt won't *let* me forget it; she will always be asking "Have the Tarringtons had their mice?" and questions of that sort. She says if you keep wild creatures in captivity you ought to see after their wants, and of course she's quite right there.'

'I met you at luncheon at your aunt's house once——' broke in Mr. Tarrington, pale but still resolute.

'My aunt never lunches,' said Clovis; 'she belongs to the National Anti-Luncheon League, which is doing quite a lot of good work in a quiet, unobtrusive way. A subscription of half a crown per quarter entitles you to go without ninety-two luncheons.'

'This must be something new,' exclaimed Tarrington.

'It's the same aunt that I've always had,' said Clovis coldly.

'I perfectly well remember meeting you at a luncheon-party given by your aunt,' persisted Tarrington, who was beginning to flush an unhealthy shade of mottled pink.

'What was there for lunch?' asked Clovis.

'Oh, well, I don't remember that——'

'How nice of you to remember my aunt when you can no longer recall the names of the things you ate. Now my memory works quite differently. I can remember a menu long after I've forgotten the hostess that accompanied it. When I was seven years old I recollect being given a peach at a garden-party by some Duchess or other; I can't remember a thing about her, except that I imagine our acquaintance must have been of the slightest, as she called me a " nice little boy," but I have unfading memories of that peach. It was one of those exuberant peaches that meet you half-way, so to speak, and are all over you in a moment. It was a beautiful unspoiled product of a hothouse, and yet it managed quite successfully to give itself the airs of a compôte. You had to bite it and imbibe it at the same time. To me there has always been something charming and mystic in the thought of that delicate velvet globe of fruit, slowly ripening and warming to perfection through the long summer days and perfumed nights, and then coming suddenly athwart my life in the supreme moment of its existence. I can never forget it, even if I wished to. And when I had devoured all that was edible of it, there still remained the stone, which a heedless, thoughtless child would doubtless have thrown away; I put it down the neck of a young friend who was wearing a very *décolleté* sailor suit. I told him it was a scorpion, and from the way he wriggled and screamed he evidently believed it, though where the silly kid imagined I could procure a live scorpion at a garden-party I don't know. Altogether, that peach is for me an unfading and happy memory——'

The defeated Tarrington had by this time retreated out of ear-shot, comforting himself as best he might with the reflection that a picnic which included the presence of Clovis might prove a doubtfully agreeable experience.

' I shall certainly go in for a Parliamentary career,' said Clovis to himself as he turned complacently to rejoin his aunt. ' As a talker-out of inconvenient bills I should be invaluable.'

THE HOUNDS OF FATE

IN the fading light of a close dull autumn afternoon Martin Stoner plodded his way along muddy lanes and rut-seamed cart tracks that led he knew not exactly whither. Somewhere in front of him, he fancied, lay the sea, and towards the sea his footsteps seemed persistently turning; why he was struggling wearily forward to that goal he could scarcely have explained, unless he was possessed by the same instinct that turns a hard-pressed stag cliffward in its last extremity. In his case the hounds of Fate were certainly pressing him with unrelenting insistence; hunger, fatigue, and despairing hopelessness had numbed his brain, and he could scarcely summon sufficient energy to wonder what underlying impulse was driving him onward. Stoner was one of those unfortunate individuals who seem to have tried everything; a natural slothfulness and improvidence had always intervened to blight any chance of even moderate success, and now he was at the end of his tether, and there was nothing more to try. Desperation had not awakened in him any dormant reserve of energy; on the contrary, a mental torpor grew up round the crisis of his fortunes. With the clothes he stood up in, a halfpenny in his pocket, and no single friend or acquaintance to turn to, with no prospect either of a bed for the night or a meal for the morrow, Martin Stoner trudged stolidly forward, between moist hedgerows and beneath dripping trees, his mind almost a blank, except that he was subconsciously aware that somewhere in front of him lay the sea. Another consciousness obtruded itself now and then—the knowledge that he was miserably hungry. Presently he came to a halt by an open gateway that led into a spacious and rather neglected farm-garden; there was little sign of life about, and the farm-house at the further end of the garden looked chill and inhospitable. A drizzling rain, however, was setting in, and Stoner thought that here perhaps he might obtain a few minutes' shelter and buy a glass of milk with his last remaining coin. He turned slowly and wearily into the garden and followed a narrow, flagged path up to a side door. Before he had time to knock the door opened and a bent, withered-looking old man stood aside in the doorway as though to let him pass in.

' Could I come in out of the rain? ' Stoner began, but the old man interrupted him.

' Come in, Master Tom. I knew you would come back one of these days."

Stoner lurched across the threshold and stood staring uncomprehendingly at the other.

' Sit down while I put you out a bit of supper,' said the old man with quavering eagerness. Stoner's legs gave way from very weariness, and he sank inertly into the arm-chair that had been pushed up to him. In another minute he was devouring the cold meat, cheese, and bread, that had been placed on the table at his side.

' You'm little changed these four years,' went on the old man, in a voice that sounded to Stoner as something in a dream, far away and inconsequent; ' but you'll find us a deal changed, you will. There's no one about the place same as when you left; nought but me and your old Aunt. I'll go and tell her that you'm come; she won't be seeing you, but she'll let you stay right enough. She always did say if you was to come back you should stay, but she'd never set eyes on you or speak to you again.'

The old man placed a mug of beer on the table in front of Stoner and then hobbled away down a long passage. The drizzle of rain had changed to a furious lashing downpour, which beat violently against door and windows. The wanderer thought with a shudder of what the sea-shore must look like under this drenching rainfall, with night beating down on all sides. He finished the food and beer and sat numbly waiting for the return of his strange host. As the minutes ticked by on the grandfather clock in the corner a new hope began to flicker and grow in the young man's mind; it was merely the expansion of his former craving for food and a few minutes' rest into a longing to find a night's shelter under this seemingly hospitable roof. A clattering of footsteps down the passage heralded the old farm servant's return.

'The old missus won't see you, Master Tom, but she says you are to stay. 'Tis right enough, seeing the farm will be yours when she be put under earth. I've had a fire lit in your room, Master Tom, and the maids has put fresh sheets on to the bed. You'll find nought changed up there. Maybe you'm tired and would like to go there now.'

Without a word Martin Stoner rose heavily to his feet and followed his ministering angel along a passage, up a short creaking stair, along another passage, and into a large room lit with a cheerfully blazing fire. There was but little furniture, plain, old-fashioned, and good of its kind; a stuffed squirrel in a case and a wall-calendar of four years ago were about the only symptoms of decoration. But Stoner had eyes for little else than the bed, and could scarce wait to tear his clothes off him before rolling in a luxury of weariness into its comfortable depths. The hounds of Fate seemed to have checked for a brief moment.

In the cold light of morning Stoner laughed mirthlessly as he slowly realized the position in which he found himself. Perhaps he might snatch a bit of breakfast on the strength of his likeness to this other missing ne'er-do-well, and get safely away before anyone discovered the fraud that had been thrust on him. In the room downstairs he found the bent old man ready with a dish of bacon and fried eggs for 'Master Tom's' breakfast, while a hard-faced elderly maid brought in a teapot and poured him out a cup of tea. As he sat at the table a small spaniel came up and made friendly advances.

''Tis old Bowker's pup,' exclaimed the old man, whom the hard-faced maid had addressed as George. ' She was main fond of you; never seemed the same after you went away to Australee. She died 'bout a year agone. 'Tis her pup.'

Stoner found it difficult to regret her decease; as a witness for identification she would have left something to be desired.

'You'll go for a ride, Master Tom?' was the next startling proposition that came from the old man. 'We've a nice little roan cob that goes well in saddle. Old Biddy is getting a bit up in years, though 'er goes well still, but I'll have the little roan saddled and brought round to door.'

'I've got no riding things,' stammered the castaway, almost laughing as he looked down at his one suit of well-worn clothes.

'Master Tom,' said the old man earnestly, almost with an offended air, 'all your things is just as you left them. A bit of airing before the fire an' they'll be all right. 'Twill be a bit of a distraction like, a little riding and wild-fowling now and agen. You'll find the folk around here has hard and bitter minds towards you. They hasn't forgotten nor forgiven. No one'll come nigh you, so you'd best get what distraction you can with horse and dog. They'm good company, too.'

Old George hobbled away to give his orders, and Stoner, feeling more than ever like one in a dream, went upstairs to inspect 'Master Tom's' wardrobe. A ride was one of the pleasures dearest to his heart, and there was some protection against immediate discovery of his imposture in the thought that none of Tom's aforetime companions were likely to favour him with a close inspection. As the interloper thrust himself into some tolerably well-fitting riding cords he wondered vaguely what manner of misdeed the genuine Tom had committed to set the whole countryside against him. The thud of quick, eager hoofs on damp earth cut short his speculations. The roan cob had been brought up to the side door.

'Talk of beggars on horseback,' thought Stoner to himself, as he trotted rapidly along the muddy lanes where he had tramped yesterday as a down-at-heel outcast; and then he flung reflection indolently aside and gave himself up to the pleasure of a smart canter along the turf-grown side of a level stretch of road. At an open gateway he checked his pace to allow two carts to turn into a field. The lads driving the carts found time to give him a prolonged stare, and as he passed on he heard an excited voice call out, ' 'Tis Tom Prike! I knowed him at once; showing hisself here agen, is he? '

Evidently the likeness which had imposed at close quarters on a doddering old man was good enough to mislead younger eyes at a short distance.

In the course of his ride he met with ample evidence to confirm the statement that local folk had neither forgotten nor forgiven the bygone crime which had come to him as a legacy from the absent Tom. Scowling looks, mutterings, and nudgings greeted him whenever he chanced upon human beings; ' Bowker's pup,' trotting placidly by his side, seemed the one element of friendliness in a hostile world.

As he dismounted at the side door he caught a fleeting glimpse of a gaunt, elderly woman peering at him from behind the curtain of an upper window. Evidently this was his aunt by adoption.

Over the ample midday meal that stood in readiness for him Stoner was able to review the possibilities of his extraordinary situation. The real Tom, after four years of absence, might suddenly turn up at the farm, or a letter might come from him at any moment. Again, in the character of heir to the farm, the false Tom might be called on to sign documents, which would be an embarrassing predicament. Or a relative might arrive who would not imitate the aunt's attitude of aloofness. All these things would mean ignominious exposure. On the other hand, the alternative was the open sky and the muddy lanes that led down to the sea. The farm offered him, at any rate, a temporary refuge from destitution; farming was one of the many things he had ' tried,' and he would be able to do a certain amount of work in return for the hospitality to which he was so little entitled.

' Will you have cold pork for your supper,' asked the hard-faced maid, as she cleared the table, ' or will you have it hotted up? '

' Hot, with onions,' said Stoner. It was the only time in his

E (547)

life that he had made a rapid decision.   And as he gave the order he knew that he meant to stay.

Stoner kept rigidly to those portions of the house which seemed to have been allotted to him by a tacit treaty of delimitation.   When he took part in the farm-work it was as one who worked under orders and never initiated them.   Old George, the roan cob, and Bowker's pup were his sole companions in a world that was otherwise frostily silent and hostile.   Of the mistress of the farm he saw nothing.   Once, when he knew she had gone forth to church, he made a furtive visit to the farm parlour in an endeavour to glean some fragmentary knowledge of the young man whose place he had usurped, and whose ill-repute he had fastened on himself.   There were many photographs hung on the walls, or stuck in prim frames, but the likeness he sought for was not among them.   At last, in an album thrust out of sight, he came across what he wanted.   There was a whole series, labelled ' Tom,' a podgy child of three, in a fantastic frock, an awkward boy of about twelve, holding a cricket bat as though he loathed it, a rather good-looking youth of eighteen with very smooth, evenly parted hair, and, finally, a young man with a somewhat surly dare-devil expression. At this last portrait Stoner looked with particular interest; the likeness to himself was unmistakable.

From the lips of old George, who was garrulous enough on most subjects, he tried again and again to learn something of the nature of the offence which shut him off as a creature to be shunned and hated by his fellow-men.

' What do the folk around here say about me ? ' he asked one day as they were walking home from an outlying field.

The old man shook his head.

' They be bitter agen you, mortal bitter.   Aye, 'tis a sad business, a sad business.'

And never could he be got to say anything more enlightening.

On a clear frosty evening, a few days before the festival of Christmas, Stoner stood in a corner of the orchard which commanded a wide view of the countryside.   Here and there he could see the twinkling dots of lamp or candle glow which told of human homes where the goodwill and jollity of the season held their sway.   Behind him lay the grim, silent farm-house, where no one ever laughed, where even a quarrel would have seemed cheerful.   As he turned to look at the long grey front of the gloom-shadowed building, a door opened and old George came hurriedly forth.   Stoner heard his adopted name called in a tone of strained anxiety.   Instantly he knew that something untoward had happened, and with a quick revulsion of outlook his sanctuary became in his eyes a place of peace and contentment, from which he dreaded to be driven.

'Master Tom,' said the old man in a hoarse whisper, 'you must slip away quiet from here for a few days.   Michael Ley is back in the village, an' he swears to shoot you if he can come across you.   He'll do it, too, there's murder in the look of him.   Get away under cover of night, 'tis only for a week or so, he won't be here longer.'

'But where am I to go?' stammered Stoner, who had caught the infection of the old man's obvious terror.

'Go right away along the coast to Punchford and keep hid there.   When Michael's safe gone I'll ride the roan over to the Green Dragon at Punchford; when you see the cob stabled at the Green Dragon 'tis a sign you may come back agen.'

'But——' began Stoner hesitatingly.

''Tis all right for money,' said the other; 'the old Missus agrees you'd best do as I say, and she's given me this.'

The old man produced three sovereigns and some odd silver.

Stoner felt more of a cheat than ever as he stole away that night from the back gate of the farm with the old woman's money in his pocket.   Old George and Bowker's pup stood watching him a silent farewell from the yard.   He could scarcely fancy that he would ever come back, and he felt a throb of compunction for those two humble friends who would wait wistfully for his return.   Some day perhaps the real Tom would come back, and there would be wild wonderment among those simple farm folks as to the identity of the shadowy guest they had harboured under their roof.   For his own fate he felt no immediate anxiety; three pounds goes but little way in the world when there is nothing behind it, but to a man who has counted his exchequer in pennies it seems a good starting-point.   Fortune had done him a whimsically kind turn when last he trod these lanes as a hopeless adventurer, and there might be yet a chance of his finding some work and making a fresh start; as he got further from the farm his spirits rose higher.   There was a sense of relief in regaining once more his lost identity and ceasing to be the uneasy ghost of another. He scarcely bothered to speculate about the implacable enemy who had dropped from nowhere into his life; since that life was now behind him one unreal item the more made little difference.   For the first time for many months he began to hum a careless light-hearted refrain.   Then there stepped out from the shadow of an overhanging oak tree a man with a gun.   There was no need to wonder who he might be; the moonlight falling on his white set face revealed a glare of human hate such as Stoner in the ups and downs of his wanderings had never seen before.   He sprang aside in a wild effort to break through the hedge that bordered the lane, but the tough branches held him fast.   The hounds of Fate had waited for him in those narrow lanes, and this time they were not to be denied.

THE RECESSIONAL

CLOVIS sat in the hottest zone but two of a Turkish bath, alternately inert in statuesque contemplation and rapidly manœuvring a fountain-pen over the pages of a note-book.

'Don't interrupt me with your childish prattle,' he observed to Bertie van Tahn, who had slung himself languidly into a neighbouring chair and looked conversationally inclined; 'I'm writing deathless verse.'

Bertie looked interested.

'I say, what a boon you would be to portrait painters if you really got to be notorious as a poetry writer. If they couldn't get your likeness hung in the Academy as " Clovis Sangrail, Esq., at work on his latest poem," they could slip you in as a Study of the Nude or Orpheus descending into Jermyn Street. They always complain that modern dress handicaps them, whereas a towel and a fountain-pen——'

'It was Mrs. Packletide's suggestion that I should write this thing,' said Clovis, ignoring the bypaths to fame that Bertie van Tahn was pointing out to him. 'You see, Loona Bimberton had a Coronation Ode accepted by the *New Infancy*, a paper that has been started with the idea of making the *New Age* seem elderly and hidebound. "So clever of you, dear Loona," the Packletide remarked when she had read it; " of course, anyone could write a Coronation Ode, but no one else would have thought of doing it." Loona protested that these things were extremely difficult to do, and gave us to understand that they were more or less the province of a gifted few. Now the Packletide has been rather decent to me in many ways, a sort of financial ambulance, you know, that carries you off the field when you're hard hit, which is a frequent occurrence with me, and I've no use whatever for Loona Bimberton, so I chipped in and said I could turn out that sort of stuff by the square yard if I gave my mind to it. Loona said I couldn't, and we got bets on, and between you and me I think the money's fairly safe. Of course, one of the conditions of the wager is that the thing has to be published in something or other, local newspapers barred; but Mrs. Packletide has endeared herself by many little acts of thoughtfulness to the editor of the *Smoky Chimney*, so if I can hammer out anything at all approaching the level of the usual Ode output we ought to be all right. So far I'm getting along so comfortably that I begin to be afraid that I must be one of the gifted few.'

' It's rather late in the day for a Coronation Ode, isn't it? ' said Bertie.

' Of course,' said Clovis; ' this is going to be a Durbar Recessional, the sort of thing that you can keep by you for all time if you want to.'

' Now I understand your choice of a place to write it in,' said Bertie van Tahn, with the air of one who has suddenly unravelled a hitherto obscure problem; ' you want to get the local temperature.'

' I came here to get freedom from the inane interruptions of the mentally deficient,' said Clovis, ' but it seems I asked too much of fate.'

Bertie van Tahn prepared to use his towel as a weapon of precision, but reflecting that he had a good deal of unprotected coast-line himself, and that Clovis was equipped with a fountain-pen as well as a towel, he relapsed pacifically into the depths of his chair.

' May one hear extracts from the immortal work? ' he asked. ' I promise that nothing that I hear now shall prejudice me against borrowing a copy of the *Smoky Chimney* at the right moment.'

' It's rather like casting pearls into a trough,' remarked Clovis pleasantly, ' but I don't mind reading you bits of it. It begins with a general dispersal of the Durbar participants :

> " Back to their homes in Himalayan heights
> The stale pale elephants of Cutch Behar
> Roll like great galleons on a tideless sea——" '

' I don't believe Cutch Behar is anywhere near the Himalayan region,' interrupted Bertie. ' You ought to have an atlas on hand when you do this sort of thing; and why stale and pale?'

' After the late hours and the excitement, of course,' said Clovis; ' and I said their *homes* were in the Himalayas. You can have Himalayan elephants in Cutch Behar, I suppose, just as you have Irish-bred horses running at Ascot.'

' You said they were going back to the Himalayas,' objected Bertie.

' Well, they would naturally be sent home to recuperate. It's the usual thing out there to turn elephants loose in the hills, just as we put horses out to grass in this country.'

Clovis could at least flatter himself that he had infused some of the reckless splendour of the East into his mendacity.

' Is it all going to be in blank verse?' asked the critic.

' Of course not; " Durbar " comes at the end of the fourth line.'

' That seems so cowardly; however, it explains why you pitched on Cutch Behar.'

' There is more connection between geographical place-names and poetical inspiration than is generally recognized; one of the chief reasons why there are so few really great poems about Russia in our language is that you can't possibly get a rhyme to names like Smolensk and Tobolsk and Minsk.'

Clovis spoke with the authority of one who has tried.

' Of course, you could rhyme Omsk with Tomsk,' he continued; ' in fact, they seem to be there for that purpose, but the public wouldn't stand that sort of thing indefinitely.'

' The public will stand a good deal,' said Bertie malevolently, ' and so small a proportion of it knows Russian that you could always have an explanatory footnote asserting that the last three letters in Smolensk are not pronounced. It's quite as believable as your statement about putting elephants out to grass in the Himalayan range.'

' I've got rather a nice bit,' resumed Clovis with unruffled serenity, ' giving an evening scene on the outskirts of a jungle village :

> " Where the coiled cobra in the gloaming gloats,
>   And prowling panthers stalk the wary goats." '

' There is practically no gloaming in tropical countries,' said Bertie indulgently; ' but I like the masterly reticence with which you treat the cobra's motive for gloating. The unknown is proverbially the uncanny. I can picture nervous readers of the *Smoky Chimney* keeping the light turned on in their bedrooms all night out of sheer sickening uncertainty as to *what* the cobra might have been gloating about.'

' Cobras gloat naturally,' said Clovis, ' just as wolves are always ravening from mere force of habit, even after they've hopelessly overeaten themselves. I've got a fine bit of colour painting later on,' he added, ' where I describe the dawn coming up over the Brahmaputra river :

> " The amber dawn-drenched East with sun-shafts kissed,
>   Stained sanguine apricot and amethyst,
>   O'er the washed emerald of the mango groves
>   Hangs in a mist of opalescent mauves,
>   While painted parrot-flights impinge the haze
>   With scarlet, chalcedon and chrysoprase." '

' I've never seen the dawn come up over the Brahmaputra river,' said Bertie, ' so I can't say if it's a good description of the event, but it sounds more like an account of an extensive jewel robbery. Anyhow, the parrots give a good useful touch of local colour. I suppose you've introduced some tigers into the scenery? An Indian landscape would have rather a bare, unfinished look without a tiger or two in the middle distance.'

' I've got a hen-tiger somewhere in the poem,' said Clovis, hunting through his notes. ' Here she is :

" The tawny tigress 'mid the tangled teak
   Drags to her purring cubs' enraptured ears
   The harsh death-rattle in the pea-fowl's beak,
   A jungle lullaby of blood and tears." '

Bertie van Tahn rose hurriedly from his recumbent position and made for the glass door leading into the next compartment.

' I think your idea of home life in the jungle is perfectly horrid,' he said. ' The cobra was sinister enough, but the improvised rattle in the tiger-nursery is the limit. If you're going to make me turn hot and cold all over I may as well go into the steam room at once.'

' Just listen to this line,' said Clovis; ' it would make the reputation of any ordinary poet:

                     " and overhead
The pendulum-patient Punkah, parent of stillborn breeze." '

' Most of your readers will think " punkah " is a kind of iced drink or half-time at polo,' said Bertie, and disappeared into the steam.

     .   .   .   .   .

The *Smoky Chimney* duly published the ' Recessional,' but it proved to be its swan song, for the paper never attained to another issue.

Loona Bimberton gave up her intention of attending the Durbar and went into a nursing-home on the Sussex Downs. Nervous breakdown after a particularly strenuous season was the usually accepted explanation, but there are three or four people who know that she never really recovered from the dawn breaking over the Brahmaputra river.

A MATTER OF SENTIMENT

IT was the eve of the great race, and scarcely a member of Lady Susan's house-party had as yet a single bet on. It was one of those unsatisfactory years when one horse held a commanding market position, not by reason of any general belief in its crushing superiority, but because it was extremely difficult to pitch on any other candidate to whom to pin one's faith. Peradventure II was the favourite, not in the sense of being a popular fancy, but by virtue of a lack of confidence in any one of his rather undistinguished rivals. The brains of clubland were much exercised in seeking out possible merit where none was very obvious to the naked intelligence, and the house-party at Lady Susan's was possessed by the same uncertainty and irresolution that infected wider circles.

' It is just the time for bringing off a good coup,' said Bertie van Tahn.

' Undoubtedly. But with what? ' demanded Clovis for the twentieth time.

The women of the party were just as keenly interested in the matter, and just as helplessly perplexed; even the mother of Clovis, who usually got good racing information from her dressmaker, confessed herself fancy free on this occasion. Colonel Drake, who was professor of military history at a minor cramming establishment, was the only person who had a definite selection for the event, but as his choice varied every three hours he was worse than useless as an inspired guide. The crowning difficulty of the problem was that it could only be fitfully and furtively discussed. Lady Susan disapproved of racing. She disapproved of many things; some people went as far as to say that she disapproved of most things. Disapproval was to her what neuralgia and fancy needlework are to many other women. She disapproved of early morning tea and auction bridge, of ski-ing and the two-step, of the

Russian ballet and the Chelsea Arts Club ball, of the French policy in Morocco and the British policy everywhere. It was not that she was particularly strict or narrow in her views of life, but she had been the eldest sister of a large family of self-indulgent children, and her particular form of indulgence had consisted in openly disapproving of the foibles of the others. Unfortunately the hobby had grown up with her. As she was rich, influential, and very, very kind, most people were content to count their early tea as well lost on her behalf. Still, the necessity for hurriedly dropping the discussion of an enthralling topic, and suppressing all mention of it during her presence on the scene, was an affliction at a moment like the present, when time was slipping away and indecision was the prevailing note.

After a lunch-time of rather strangled and uneasy conversation, Clovis managed to get most of the party together at the further end of the kitchen gardens, on the pretext of admiring the Himalayan pheasants. He had made an important discovery. Motkin, the butler, who (as Clovis expressed it) had grown prematurely grey in Lady Susan's service, added to his other excellent qualities an intelligent interest in matters connected with the Turf. On the subject of the forthcoming race he was not illuminating, except in so far that he shared the prevailing unwillingness to see a winner in Peradventure II. But where he outshone all the members of the house-party was in the fact that he had a second cousin who was head stable-lad at a neighbouring racing establishment, and usually gifted with much inside information as to private form and possibilities. Only the fact of her ladyship having taken it into her head to invite a house-party for the last week of May had prevented Mr. Motkin from paying a visit of consultation to his relative with respect to the big race; there was still time to cycle over if he could get leave of absence for the afternoon on some specious excuse.

'Let's jolly well hope he does,' said Bertie van Tahn; 'under the circumstances a second cousin is almost as useful as second sight.'

'That stable ought to know something, if knowledge is to be found anywhere,' said Mrs. Packletide hopefully.

'I expect you'll find he'll echo my fancy for Motorboat,' said Colonel Drake.

At this moment the subject had to be hastily dropped. Lady Susan bore down upon them, leaning on the arm of Clovis's mother, to whom she was confiding the fact that she disapproved of the craze for Pekingese spaniels. It was the third thing she had found to time disapprove of since lunch, without counting her silent and permanent disapproval of the way Clovis's mother did her hair.

'We have been admiring the Himalayan pheasants,' said Mrs. Packletide suavely.

'They went off to a bird-show at Nottingham early this morning,' said Lady Susan, with the air of one who disapproves of hasty and ill-considered lying.

'Their house, I mean; such perfect roosting arrangements, and all so clean,' resumed Mrs. Packletide, with an increased glow of enthusiasm. The odious Bertie van Tahn was murmuring audible prayers for Mrs. Packletide's ultimate estrangement from the paths of falsehood.

'I hope you don't mind dinner being a quarter of an hour late to-night,' said Lady Susan; 'Motkin has had an urgent summons to go and see a sick relative this afternoon. He wanted to bicycle there, but I am sending him in the motor.'

'How very kind of you! Of course we don't mind dinner being put off.' The assurances came with unanimous and hearty sincerity.

At the dinner-table that night an undercurrent of furtive curiosity directed itself towards Motkin's impassive countenance. One or two of the guests almost expected to find a slip of paper concealed in their napkins, bearing the name of the second cousin's selection. They had not long to wait. As the butler went round with the murmured question, 'Sherry?' he added in an even lower tone the cryptic words, 'Better not.' Mrs. Packletide gave a start of alarm, and refused the sherry;

there seemed some sinister suggestion in the butler's warning, as though her hostess had suddenly become addicted to the Borgia habit. A moment later the explanation flashed on her that ' Better Not ' was the name of one of the runners in the big race. Clovis was already pencilling it on his cuff, and Colonel Drake, in his turn, was signalling to every one in hoarse whispers and dumbshow the fact that he had all along fancied ' B.N.'

Early next morning a sheaf of telegrams went Townward, representing the market commands of the house-party and servants' hall.

It was a wet afternoon, and most of Lady Susan's guests hung about the hall, waiting apparently for the appearance of tea, though it was scarcely yet due. The advent of a telegram quickened every one into a flutter of expectancy; the page who brought the telegram to Clovis waited with unusual alertness to know if there might be an answer.

Clovis read the message and gave an exclamation of annoyance.

' No bad news, I hope,' said Lady Susan. Every one else knew that the news was not good.

' It's only the result of the Derby,' he blurted out; ' Sadowa won; an utter outsider.'

' Sadowa ! ' exclaimed Lady Susan; ' you don't say so ! How remarkable ! It's the first time I've ever backed a horse; in fact I disapprove of horse-racing, but just for once in a way I put money on this horse, and it's gone and won.'

' May I ask,' said Mrs. Packletide, amid the general silence, ' why you put your money on this particular horse? None of the sporting prophets mentioned it as having an outside chance.'

' Well,' said Lady Susan, ' you may laugh at me, but it was the name that attracted me. You see, I was always mixed up with the Franco-German war; I was married on the day that the war was declared, and my eldest child was born the day that peace was signed, so anything connected with the war has always interested me. And when I saw there was a horse running in the Derby called after one of the battles in the Franco-German war, I said I *must* put some money on it, for once in a way, though I disapprove of racing. And it's actually won.'

There was a general groan. No one groaned more deeply than the professor of military history.

THE SECRET SIN OF
SEPTIMUS BROPE

'Who and what is Mr. Brope?' demanded the aunt of Clovis suddenly.

Mrs. Riversedge, who had been snipping off the heads of defunct roses, and thinking of nothing in particular, sprang hurriedly to mental attention. She was one of those old-fashioned hostesses who consider that one ought to know something about one's guests, and that the something ought to be to their credit.

'I believe he comes from Leighton Buzzard,' she observed by way of preliminary explanation.

'In these days of rapid and convenient travel,' said Clovis, who was dispersing a colony of green-fly with visitations of cigarette smoke, 'to come from Leighton Buzzard does not necessarily denote any great strength of character. It might only mean mere restlessness. Now if he had left it under a cloud, or as a protest against the incurable and heartless frivolity of its inhabitants, that would tell us something about the man and his mission in life.'

'What does he do?' pursued Mrs. Troyle magisterially.

'He edits the *Cathedral Monthly*,' said her hostess, 'and he's enormously learned about memorial brasses and transepts and the influence of Byzantine worship on modern liturgy, and all those sort of things. Perhaps he is just a little bit heavy and immersed in one range of subjects, but it takes all sorts to make a good house-party, you know. You don't find him *too* dull, do you?'

'Dullness I could overlook,' said the aunt of Clovis; 'what I cannot forgive is his making love to my maid.'

'My dear Mrs. Troyle,' gasped the hostess, 'what an extraordinary idea! I assure you Mr. Brope would not dream of doing such a thing.'

'His dreams are a matter of indifference to me; for all I care his slumbers may be one long indiscretion of unsuitable erotic advances, in which the entire servants' hall may be involved. But in his waking hours he shall not make love to my maid. It's no use arguing about it, I'm firm on the point.'

'But you must be mistaken,' persisted Mrs. Riversedge; 'Mr. Brope would be the last person to do such a thing.'

'He is the first person to do such a thing, as far as my information goes, and if I have any voice in the matter he certainly shall be the last. Of course, I am not referring to respectably-intentioned lovers.'

'I simply cannot think that a man who writes so charmingly and informingly about transepts and Byzantine influences would behave in such an unprincipled manner,' said Mrs. Riversedge; 'what evidence have you that he's doing anything of the sort? I don't want to doubt your word, of course, but we mustn't be too ready to condemn him unheard, must we?'

'Whether we condemn him or not, he has certainly not been unheard. He has the room next to my dressing-room, and on two occasions, when I dare say he thought I was absent, I have plainly heard him announcing through the wall, "I love you, Florrie." Those partition walls upstairs are very thin; one can almost hear a watch ticking in the next room.'

'Is your maid called Florence?'

'Her name is Florinda.'

'What an extraordinary name to give a maid!'

'I did not give it to her; she arrived in my service already christened.'

'What I mean is,' said Mrs. Riversedge, 'that when I get maids with unsuitable names I call them Jane; they soon get used to it.'

'An excellent plan,' said the aunt of Clovis coldly; 'unfortunately I have got used to being called Jane myself. It happens to be my name.'

She cut short Mrs. Riversedge's flood of apologies by abruptly remarking:

'The question is not whether I'm to call my maid Florinda, but whether Mr. Brope is to be permitted to call her Florrie. I am strongly of opinion than he shall not.'

'He may have been repeating the words of some song,' said Mrs. Riversedge hopefully; 'there are lots of those sorts of silly refrains with girls' names,' she continued, turning to Clovis as a possible authority on the subject. '"You mustn't call me Mary——"'

'I shouldn't think of doing so,' Clovis assured her; 'in the first place, I've always understood that your name was Henrietta; and then I hardly know you well enough to take such a liberty.'

'I mean there's a *song* with that refrain,' hurriedly explained Mrs. Riversedge, ' and there's " Rhoda, Rhoda kept a pagoda," and " Maisie is a daisy," and heaps of others. Certainly it doesn't sound like Mr. Brope to be singing such songs, but I think we ought to give him the benefit of the doubt.'

'I had already done so,' said Mrs. Troyle, 'until further evidence came my way.'

She shut her lips with the resolute finality of one who enjoys the blessed certainty of being implored to open them again.

'Further evidence!' exclaimed her hostess; 'do tell me!'

'As I was coming upstairs after breakfast Mr. Brope was just passing my room. In the most natural way in the world a piece of paper dropped out of a packet that he held in his hand and fluttered to the ground just at my door. I was going to call out to him " You've dropped something," and then for some reason I held back and didn't show myself till he was safely in his room. You see it occurred to me that I was very seldom in my room just at that hour, and that Florinda was almost always there tidying up things about that time. So I picked up that innocent-looking piece of paper.'

Mrs. Troyle paused again, with the self-applauding air of one who has detected an asp lurking in an apple-charlotte.

Mrs. Riversedge snipped vigorously at the nearest rose bush, incidentally decapitating a Viscountess Folkstone that was just coming into bloom.

'What was on the paper?' she asked.

'Just the words in pencil, "I love you, Florrie," and then underneath, crossed out with a faint line, but perfectly plain to read, "Meet me in the garden by the yew."'

'There *is* a yew tree at the bottom of the garden,' admitted Mrs. Riversedge.

'At any rate he appears to be truthful,' commented Clovis.

'To think that a scandal of this sort should be going on under my roof!' said Mrs. Riversedge indignantly.

'I wonder why it is that scandal seems so much worse under a roof,' observed Clovis; 'I've always regarded it as a proof of the superior delicacy of the cat tribe that it conducts most of its scandals above the slates.'

'Now I come to think of it,' resumed Mrs. Riversedge, 'there are things about Mr. Brope that I've never been able to account for. His income, for instance: he only gets two hundred a year as editor of the *Cathedral Monthly*, and I know that his people are quite poor, and he hasn't any private means. Yet he manages to afford a flat somewhere in Westminster, and he goes abroad to Bruges and those sort of places every year, and always dresses well, and gives quite nice luncheon-parties in the season. You can't do all that on two hundred a year, can you?'

'Does he write for any other papers?' queried Mrs. Troyle.

'No, you see he specializes so entirely on liturgy and ecclesiastical architecture that his field is rather restricted. He once tried the *Sporting and Dramatic* with an article on church edifices in famous fox-hunting centres, but it wasn't considered of sufficient general interest to be accepted. No, I don't see how he can support himself in his present style merely by what he writes.'

'Perhaps he sells spurious transepts to American enthusiasts,' suggested Clovis.

' How could you sell a transept?' said Mrs. Riversedge; ' such a thing would be impossible.'

' Whatever he may do to eke out his income,' interrupted Mrs. Troyle, ' he is certainly not going to fill in his leisure moments by making love to my maid.'

' Of course not,' agreed her hostess; ' that must be put a stop to at once. But I don't quite know what we ought to do.'

' You might put a barbed wire entanglement round the yew tree as a precautionary measure,' said Clovis.

' I don't think that the disagreeable situation that has arisen is improved by flippancy,' said Mrs. Riversedge; ' a good maid is a treasure——'

' I am sure I don't know what I should do without Florinda,' admitted Mrs. Troyle; ' she understands my hair. I've long ago given up trying to do anything with it myself. I regard one's hair as I regard husbands: as long as one is seen together in public one's private divergences don't matter. Surely that was the luncheon gong.'

Septimus Brope and Clovis had the smoking-room to themselves after lunch. The former seemed restless and preoccupied, the latter quietly observant.

' What is a lorry?' asked Septimus suddenly; ' I don't mean the thing on wheels, of course I know what that is, but isn't there a bird with a name like that, the larger form of a lorikeet?'

' I fancy it's a lory, with one " r," ' said Clovis lazily, ' in which case it's no good to you.'

Septimus Brope stared in some astonishment.

' How do you mean, no good to me?' he asked, with more than a trace of uneasiness in his voice.

' Won't rhyme with Florrie,' explained Clovis briefly.

Septimus sat upright in his chair, with unmistakable alarm on his face.

' How did you find out? I mean how did you know I was trying to get a rhyme to Florrie?' he asked sharply.

' I didn't know,' said Clovis, ' I only guessed. When you wanted to turn the prosaic lorry of commerce into a feathered poem flitting through the verdure of a tropical forest, I knew you must be working up a sonnet, and Florrie was the only female name that suggested itself as rhyming with lorry.'

Septimus still looked uneasy.

' I believe you know more,' he said.

Clovis laughed quietly, but said nothing.

' How much do you know?' Septimus asked desperately.

' The yew tree in the garden,' said Clovis.

' There! I felt certain I'd dropped it somewhere. But you must have guessed something before. Look here, you have surprised my secret. You won't give me away, will you? It is nothing to be ashamed of, but it wouldn't do for the editor of the *Cathedral Monthly* to go in openly for that sort of thing, would it?'

' Well, I suppose not,' admitted Clovis.

' You see,' continued Septimus, ' I get quite a decent lot of money out of it. I could never live in the style I do on what I get as editor of the *Cathedral Monthly*.'

Clovis was even more startled than Septimus had been earlier in the conversation, but he was better skilled in repressing surprise.

' Do you mean to say you get money out of—Florrie?' he asked.

' Not out of Florrie, as yet,' said Septimus; ' in fact, I don't mind saying that I'm having a good deal of trouble over Florrie. But there are a lot of others.'

Clovis's cigarette went out.

' This is *very* interesting,' he said slowly. And then, with Septimus Brope's next words, illumination dawned on him.

' There are heaps of others; for instance:

> " Cora with the lips of coral,
>   You and I will never quarrel."

That was one of my earliest successes, and it still brings me in royalties. And then there is—" Esmeralda, when I first beheld her," and " Fair Teresa, how I love to please her," both of those have been fairly popular. And there is one rather dreadful one,' continued Septimus, flushing deep carmine, ' which has brought me in more money than any of the others:

> " Lively little Lucie
> With her naughty nez retroussé."

Of course, I loathe the whole lot of them; in fact, I'm rapidly becoming something of a woman-hater under their influence, but I can't afford to disregard the financial aspect of the matter. And at the same time you can understand that my position as an authority on ecclesiastical architecture and liturgical subjects would be weakened, if not altogether ruined, if it once got about that I was the author of " Cora with the lips of coral " and all the rest of them.'

Clovis had recovered sufficiently to ask in a sympathetic, if rather unsteady voice, what was the special trouble with ' Florrie.'

' I can't get her into lyric shape, try as I will,' said Septimus mournfully.   ' You see, one has to work in a lot of sentimental, sugary compliment with a catchy rhyme, and a certain amount of personal biography or prophecy. They've all of them got to have a long string of past successes recorded about them, or else you've got to foretell blissful things about them and yourself in the future.   For instance, there is:

> " Dainty little girlie Mavis,
> She is such a rara avis,
> All the money I can save is
> All to be for Mavis mine."

It goes to a sickening namby-pamby waltz tune, and for months nothing else was sung and hummed in Blackpool and other popular centres.'

This time Clovis's self-control broke down badly.

' Please excuse me,' he gurgled, ' but I can't help it when I remember the awful solemnity of that article of yours that you so kindly read us last night, on the Coptic Church in its relation to early Christian worship.'

Septimus groaned.

' You see how it would be,' he said; ' as soon as people knew me to be the author of that miserable sentimental twaddle, all respect for the serious labours of my life would be gone. I dare say I know more about memorial brasses than anyone living, in fact I hope one day to publish a monograph on the subject, but I should be pointed out everywhere as the man whose ditties were in the mouths of nigger minstrels along the entire coast-line of our Island home.   Can you wonder that I positively hate Florrie all the time that I'm trying to grind out sugar-coated rhapsodies about her.'

' Why not give free play to your emotions, and be brutally abusive?   An uncomplimentary refrain would have an instant success as a novelty if you were sufficiently outspoken.'

' I've never thought of that,' said Septimus, ' and I'm afraid I couldn't break away from the habit of fulsome adulation and suddenly change my style.'

' You needn't change your style in the least,' said Clovis; ' merely reverse the sentiment and keep to the inane phraseology of the thing.   If you'll do the body of the song I'll knock off the refrain, which is the thing that principally matters, I believe. I shall charge half-shares in the royalties, and throw in my silence as to your guilty secret.   In the eyes of the world you shall still be the man who has devoted his life to the study of transepts and Byzantine ritual; only sometimes, in the long winter evenings, when the wind howls drearily down the chimney and the rain beats against the windows, I shall think of you as the author of " Cora with the lips of coral."   Of course, if in sheer gratitude at my silence you like to take me for a much-needed holiday to the Adriatic or somewhere equally interesting, paying all expenses, I shouldn't dream of refusing.'

Later in the afternoon Clovis found his aunt and Mrs. River-sedge indulging in gentle exercise in the Jacobean garden.

' I've spoken to Mr. Brope about F.,' he announced.

' How splendid of you! What did he say? ' came in a quick chorus from the two ladies.

' He was quite frank and straightforward with me when he saw that I knew his secret,' said Clovis, ' and it seems that his intentions were quite serious, if slightly unsuitable. I tried to show him the impracticability of the course that he was following. He said he wanted to be understood, and he seemed to think that Florinda would excel in that requirement, but I pointed out that there were probably dozens of delicately nurtured, pure-hearted young English girls who would be capable of understanding him, while Florinda was the only person in the world who understood my aunt's hair. That rather weighed with him, for he's not really a selfish animal, if you take him in the right way, and when I appealed to the memory of his happy childish days, spent amid the daisied fields of Leighton Buzzard (I suppose daisies do grow there), he was obviously affected. Anyhow, he gave me his word that he would put Florinda absolutely out of his mind, and he has agreed to go for a short trip abroad as the best distraction for his thoughts. I am going with him as far as Ragusa. If my aunt should wish to give me a really nice scarf-pin (to be chosen by myself), as a small recognition of the very considerable service I have done her, I shouldn't dream of refusing. I'm not one of those who think that because one is abroad one can go about dressed anyhow.'

A few weeks later in Blackpool and places where they sing, the following refrain held undisputed sway:

> ' How you bore me, Florrie,
> With those eyes of vacant blue;
> You'll be very sorry, Florrie,
> If I marry you.
> Though I'm easy-goin', Florrie,
> This I swear is true,
> I'll throw you down a quarry, Florrie,
> If I marry you.'

ALTHOUGH he was scarcely yet out of his teens, the Duke of Scaw was already marked out as a personality widely differing from others of his caste and period. Not in externals; therein he conformed correctly to type. His hair was faintly reminiscent of Houbigant, and at the other end of him his shoes exhaled the right *soupçon* of harness-room; his socks compelled one's attention without losing one's respect; and his attitude in repose had just that suggestion of Whistler's mother, so becoming in the really young. It was within that the trouble lay, if trouble it could be accounted, which marked him apart from his fellows. The Duke was religious. Not in any of the ordinary senses of the word; he took small heed of High Church or Evangelical standpoints, he stood outside of all the movements and missions and cults and crusades of the day, uncaring and uninterested. Yet in a mystical-practical way of his own, which had served him unscathed and unshaken through the fickle years of boyhood, he was intensely and intensively religious. His family were naturally, though unobtrusively, distressed about it. 'I am so afraid it may affect his bridge,' said his mother.

The Duke sat in a pennyworth of chair in St. James's Park, listening to the pessimisms of Belturbet, who reviewed the existing political situation from the gloomiest of standpoints.

'Where I think you political spade-workers are so silly,' said the Duke, 'is in the misdirection of your efforts. You spend thousands of pounds of money, and Heaven knows how much dynamic force of brain power and personal energy, in trying to elect or displace this or that man, whereas you could gain your ends so much more simply by making use of the men as you find them. If they don't suit your purpose as they are transform them into something more satisfactory.'

'Do you refer to hypnotic suggestion?' asked Belturbet, with the air of one who is being trifled with.

'Nothing of the sort. Do you understand what I mean by the verb to koepenick? That is to say, to replace an authority by a spurious imitation that would carry just as much weight for the moment as the displaced original; the advantage, of course, being that the koepenick replica would do what you wanted, whereas the original does what seems best in its own eyes.'

'I suppose every public man has a double, if not two or three,' said Belturbet; 'but it would be a pretty hard task to koepenick a whole bunch of them and keep the originals out of the way.'

'There have been instances in European history of highly successful koepenickery,' said the Duke dreamily.

'Oh, of course, there have been False Dimitris and Perkin Warbecks, who imposed on the world for a time,' assented Belturbet, 'but they personated people who were dead or safely out of the way. That was a comparatively simple matter. It would be far easier to pass oneself off as dead Hannibal than as living Haldane, for instance.'

'I was thinking,' said the Duke, 'of the most famous case of all, the angel who koepenicked King Robert of Sicily with such brilliant results. Just imagine what an advantage it would be to have angels deputizing, to use a horrible but convenient word, for Quinston and Lord Hugo Sizzle, for example. How much smoother the Parliamentary machine would work than at present!'

'Now you're talking nonsense,' said Belturbet; 'angels don't exist nowadays, at least, not in that way, so what is the use of dragging them into a serious discussion? It's merely silly.'

'If you talk to me like that I shall just *do* it,' said the Duke.

'Do what?' asked Belturbet. There were times when his young friend's uncanny remarks rather frightened him.

'I shall summon angelic forces to take over some of the

more troublesome personalities of our public life, and I shall send the ousted originals into temporary retirement in suitable animal organisms. It's not every one who would have the knowledge or the power necessary to bring such a thing off——'

'Oh, stop that inane rubbish,' said Belturbet angrily; 'it's getting wearisome. Here's Quinston coming,' he added, as there approached along the almost deserted path the well-known figure of a young Cabinet Minister, whose personality evoked a curious mixture of public interest and unpopularity.

'Hurry along, my dear man,' said the young Duke to the Minister, who had given him a condescending nod; 'your time is running short,' he continued in a provocative strain; 'the whole inept crowd of you will shortly be swept away into the world's waste-paper basket.'

'You poor little strawberry-leafed nonentity,' said the Minister, checking himself for a moment in his stride and rolling out his words spasmodically; 'who is going to sweep us away, I should like to know? The voting masses are on our side, and all the ability and administrative talent is on our side too. No power of earth or Heaven is going to move us from our place till we choose to quit it. No power of earth or——'

Belturbet saw, with bulging eyes, a sudden void where a moment earlier had been a Cabinet Minister; a void emphasized rather than relieved by the presence of a puffed-out bewildered-looking sparrow, which hopped about for a moment in a dazed fashion and then fell to a violent cheeping and scolding.

'If we could understand sparrow-language,' said the Duke serenely, 'I fancy we should hear something infinitely worse than "strawberry-leafed nonentity."'

'But good Heavens, Eugène,' said Belturbet hoarsely, 'what has become of—— Why, there he is! How on earth did he get there?' And he pointed with a shaking finger towards a semblance of the vanished Minister, which approached once more along the unfrequented path.

The Duke laughed.

'It is Quinston to all outward appearance,' he said composedly, 'but I fancy you will find, on closer investigation, that it is an angel understudy of the real article.'

The Angel-Quinston greeted them with a friendly smile.

'How beastly happy you two look sitting there!' he said wistfully.

'I don't suppose you'd care to change places with poor little us," replied the Duke chaffingly.

'How about poor little me?' said the Angel modestly. 'I've got to run about behind the wheels of popularity, like a spotted dog behind a carriage, getting all the dust and trying to look as if I was an important part of the machine. I must seem a perfect fool to you onlookers sometimes.'

'I think you are a perfect angel,' said the Duke.

The Angel-that-had-been-Quinston smiled and passed on his way, pursued across the breadth of the Horse Guards Parade by a tiresome little sparrow that cheeped incessantly and furiously at him.

'That's only the beginning,' said the Duke complacently; 'I've made it operative with all of them, irrespective of parties.'

Belturbet made no coherent reply; he was engaged in feeling his pulse. The Duke fixed his attention with some interest on a black swan that was swimming with haughty, stiff-necked aloofness amid the crowd of lesser water-fowl that dotted the ornamental water. For all its pride of bearing, something was evidently ruffling and enraging it; in its way it seemed as angry and amazed as the sparrow had been.

At the same moment a human figure came along the pathway. Belturbet looked up apprehensively.

'Kedzon,' he whispered briefly.

'An Angel-Kedzon, if I am not mistaken,' said the Duke. 'Look, he is talking affably to a human being. That settles it."

A shabbily dressed lounger had accosted the man who had been Viceroy in the splendid East, and who still reflected in his mien some of the cold dignity of the Himalayan snow-peaks.

'Could you tell me, sir, if them white birds is storks or halbatrosses? I had an argyment——'

The cold dignity thawed at once into genial friendliness.

'Those are pelicans, my dear sir. Are you interested in birds? If you would join me in a bun and a glass of milk at the stall yonder, I could tell you some interesting things about Indian birds. Right oh! Now the hill-mynah, for instance——'

The two men disappeared in the direction of the bun stall, chatting volubly as they went, and shadowed from the other side of the railed enclosure by a black swan, whose temper seemed to have reached the limit of inarticulate rage.

Belturbet gazed in an open-mouthed wonder after the retreating couple, then transferred his attention to the infuriated swan, and finally turned with a look of scared comprehension at his young friend lolling unconcernedly in his chair. There was no longer any room to doubt what was happening. The 'silly talk' had been translated into terrifying action.

'I think a prairie oyster on the top of a stiffish brandy-and-soda might save my reason,' said Belturbet weakly, as he limped towards his club.

It was late in the day before he could steady his nerves sufficiently to glance at the evening papers. The Parliamentary report proved significant reading, and confirmed the fears that he had been trying to shake off. Mr. Ap Dave, the Chancellor, whose lively controversial style endeared him to his supporters and embittered him, politically speaking, to his opponents, had risen in his place to make an unprovoked apology for having alluded in a recent speech to certain protesting taxpayers as 'skulkers.' He had realized on reflection that they were in all probability perfectly honest in their inability to understand certain legal technicalities of the new finance laws. The House had scarcely recovered from this sensation when Lord Hugo Sizzle caused a further flutter of astonishment by going out of his way to indulge in an outspoken appreciation of the fairness, loyalty, and straightforwardness not only of the

Chancellor, but of all the members of the Cabinet. A wit had gravely suggested moving the adjournment of the House in view of the unexpected circumstances that had arisen.

Belturbet anxiously skimmed over a further item of news printed immediately below the Parliamentary report: 'Wild cat found in an exhausted condition in Palace Yard.'

'Now I wonder which of them——' he mused, and then an appalling idea came to him. 'Supposing he's put them both into the same beast!' He hurriedly ordered another prairie oyster.

Belturbet was known in his club as a strictly moderate drinker; his consumption of alcoholic stimulants that day gave rise to considerable comment.

The events of the next few days were piquantly bewildering to the world at large; to Belturbet, who knew dimly what was happening, the situation was fraught with recurring alarms. The old saying that in politics it's the unexpected that always happens received a justification that it had hitherto somewhat lacked, and the epidemic of startling personal changes of front was not wholly confined to the realm of actual politics. The eminent chocolate magnate, Sadbury, whose antipathy to the Turf and everything connected with it was a matter of general knowledge, had evidently been replaced by an Angel-Sadbury, who proceeded to electrify the public by blossoming forth as an owner of race-horses, giving as a reason his matured conviction that the sport was, after all, one which gave healthy open-air recreation to large numbers of people drawn from all classes of the community, and incidentally stimulated the important industry of horse-breeding. His colours, chocolate and cream hoops spangled with pink stars, promised to become as popular as any on the Turf. At the same time, in order to give effect to his condemnation of the evils resulting from the spread of the gambling habit among wage-earning classes, who lived for the most part from hand to mouth, he suppressed all betting news and tipsters' forecasts in the popular evening paper that was under his control. His action received instant recognition and support from the Angel-proprietor of the *Evening Views*, the principal rival evening halfpenny paper, who forthwith issued an ukase decreeing a similar ban on betting news, and in a short while the regular evening Press was purged of all mention of starting prices and probable winners. A considerable drop in the circulation of all these papers was the immediate result, accompanied, of course, by a falling-off in advertisement value, while a crop of special betting broadsheets sprang up to supply the newly-created want. Under their influence the betting habit became if anything rather more widely diffused than before. The Duke had possibly overlooked the futility of koepenicking the leaders of the nation with excellently intentioned angel understudies, while leaving the mass of the people in its original condition.

Further sensation and dislocation was caused in the Press world by the sudden and dramatic *rapprochement* which took place between the Angel-Editor of the *Scrutator* and the Angel-Editor of the *Anglian Review*, who not only ceased to criticize and disparage the tone and tendencies of each other's publication, but agreed to exchange editorships for alternating periods. Here again public support was not on the side of the angels; constant readers of the *Scrutator* complained bitterly of the strong meat which was thrust upon them at fitful intervals in place of the almost vegetarian diet to which they had become confidently accustomed; even those who were not mentally averse to strong meat as a separate course were pardonably annoyed at being supplied with it in the pages of the *Scrutator*. To be suddenly confronted with a pungent herring salad when one had attuned oneself to tea and toast, or to discover a richly truffled segment of *paté de foie* dissembled in a bowl of bread and milk, would be an experience that might upset the equanimity of the most placidly disposed mortal. An equally vehement outcry arose from the regular subscribers of the *Anglian Review*, who protested against being served from time to time with literary fare which no young person of sixteen could possibly want to devour in secret. To take infinite precautions, they complained, against the juvenile perusal of such eminently innocuous literature was like reading the Riot Act on an uninhabited island. Both reviews suffered a serious falling-off in circulation and influence. Peace hath its devastations as well as war.

The wives of noted public men formed another element of discomfiture which the young Duke had almost entirely left out of his calculations. It is sufficiently embarrassing to keep abreast of the possible wobblings and veerings-round of a human husband, who, from the strength or weakness of his personal character, may leap over or slip through the barriers which divide the parties; for this reason a merciful politician usually marries late in life, when he has definitely made up his mind on which side he wishes his wife to be socially valuable. But these trials were as nothing compared to the bewilderment caused by the Angel-husbands who seemed in some cases to have revolutionized their outlook on life in the interval between breakfast and dinner, without premonition or preparation of any kind, and apparently without realizing the least need for subsequent explanation. The temporary peace which brooded over the Parliamentary situation was by no means reproduced in the home circles of the leading statesmen and politicians. It had been frequently and extensively remarked of Mrs. Exe that she would try the patience of an angel; now the tables were reversed, and she unwittingly had an opportunity for discovering that the capacity for exasperating behaviour was not all on one side.

And then, with the introduction of the Navy Estimates, Parliamentary peace suddenly dissolved. It was the old quarrel between Ministers and the Opposition as to the adequacy or the reverse of the Government's naval programme. The Angel-Quinston and the Angel-Hugo-Sizzle contrived to keep the debates free from personalities and pinpricks, but an enormous sensation was created when the elegant lackadaisical Halfan Halfour threatened to bring up fifty thousand stalwarts to wreck the House if the Estimates were not forthwith revised on a

Two-Power basis.   It was a memorable scene when he rose in his place, in response to the scandalized shouts of his opponents, and thundered forth, 'Gentlemen, I glory in the name of Apache.'

Belturbet, who had made several fruitless attempts to ring up his young friend since the fateful morning in St. James's Park, ran him to earth one afternoon at his club, smooth and spruce and unruffled as ever.

'Tell me, what on earth have you turned Cocksley Coxon into?' Belturbet asked anxiously, mentioning the name of one of the pillars of unorthodoxy in the Anglican Church. 'I don't fancy he *believes* in angels, and if he finds an angel preaching orthodox sermons from his pulpit while he's been turned into a fox-terrier, he'll develop rabies in less than no time.'

'I rather think it was a fox-terrier,' said the Duke lazily.

Belturbet groaned heavily, and sank into a chair.

'Look here, Eugène,' he whispered hoarsely, having first looked well round to see that no one was within hearing range, 'you've got to stop it.   Consols are jumping up and down like bronchos, and that speech of Halfour's in the House last night has simply startled everybody out of their wits.   And then on the top of it, Thistlebery——'

'What has he been saying?' asked the Duke quickly.

'Nothing. That's just what's so disturbing. Every one thought it was simply inevitable that he should come out with a great epoch-making speech at this juncture, and I've just seen on the tape that he has refused to address any meetings at present, giving as a reason his opinion that something more than mere speech-making was wanted.'

The young Duke said nothing, but his eyes shone with quiet exultation.

'It's so unlike Thistlebery,' continued Belturbet; 'at least,' he said suspiciously, 'it's unlike the *real* Thistlebery——'

'The real Thistlebery is flying about somewhere as a vocally-industrious lapwing,' said the Duke calmly; 'I expect great things of the Angel-Thistlebery,' he added.

At this moment there was a magnetic stampede of members towards the lobby, where the tape-machines were ticking out some news of more than ordinary import.

'*Coup d'état* in the North. Thistlebery seizes Edinburgh Castle. Threatens civil war unless Government expands naval programme.'

In the babel which ensued Belturbet lost sight of his young friend. For the best part of the afternoon he searched one likely haunt after another, spurred on by the sensational posters which the evening papers were displaying broadcast over the West End. 'General Baden-Baden mobilizes Boy-Scouts. Another *coup d'état* feared. Is Windsor Castle safe?' This was one of the earlier posters, and was followed by one of even more sinister purport: 'Will the Test-match have to be postponed?' It was this disquietening question which brought home the real seriousness of the situation to the London public, and made people wonder whether one might not pay too high a price for the advantages of party government. Belturbet, questing round in the hope of finding the originator of the trouble, with a vague idea of being able to induce him to restore matters to their normal human footing, came across an elderly club acquaintance who dabbled extensively in some of the more sensitive market securities. He was pale with indignation, and his pallor deepened as a breathless newsboy dashed past with a poster inscribed: 'Premier's constituency harried by moss-troopers. Halfour sends encouraging telegram to rioters. Letchworth Garden City threatens reprisals. Foreigners taking refuge in Embassies and National Liberal Club.'

'This is devil's work!' he said angrily.

Belturbet knew otherwise.

At the bottom of St. James's Street a newspaper motor-cart, which had just come rapidly along Pall Mall, was surrounded by a knot of eagerly talking people, and for the first time that afternoon Belturbet heard expressions of relief and congratulation.

It displayed a placard with the welcome announcement:

' Crisis ended.   Government gives way.   Important expansion of naval programme.'

There seemed to be no immediate necessity for pursuing the quest of the errant Duke, and Belturbet turned to make his way homeward through St. James's Park.   His mind, attuned to the alarums and excursions of the afternoon, became dimly aware that some excitement of a detached nature was going on around him.   In spite of the political ferment which reigned in the streets, quite a large crowd had gathered to watch the unfolding of a tragedy that had taken place on the shore of the ornamental water.   A large black swan, which had recently shown signs of a savage and dangerous disposition, had suddenly attacked a young gentleman who was walking by the water's edge, dragged him down under the surface, and drowned him before anyone could come to his assistance.   At the moment when Belturbet arrived on the spot several park-keepers were engaged in lifting the corpse into a punt.   Belturbet stooped to pick up a hat that lay near the scene of the struggle.   It was a smart soft felt hat, faintly reminiscent of Houbigant.

More than a month elapsed before Belturbet had sufficiently recovered from his attack of nervous prostration to take an interest once more in what was going on in the world of politics. The Parliamentary Session was still in full swing, and a General Election was looming in the near future.   He called for a batch of morning papers and skimmed rapidly through the speeches of the Chancellor, Quinston, and other Ministerial leaders, as well as those of the principal Opposition champions, and then sank back in his chair with a sigh of relief.   Evidently the spell had ceased to act after the tragedy which had overtaken its invoker.   There was no trace of angel anywhere.

THE REMOULDING OF
GROBY LINGTON

A man is known by the company he keeps

IN the morning-room of his sister-in-law's house Groby
Lington fidgeted away the passing minutes with the demure
restlessness of advanced middle age. About a quarter of an
hour would have to elapse before it would be time to say his
good-byes and make his way across the village green to the
station, with a selected escort of nephews and nieces. He
was a good-natured, kindly dispositioned man, and in theory
he was delighted to pay periodical visits to the wife and children
of his dead brother William; in practice, he infinitely preferred
the comfort and seclusion of his own house and garden, and
the companionship of his books and his parrot to these rather
meaningless and tiresome incursions into a family circle with
which he had little in common. It was not so much the spur
of his own conscience that drove him to make the occasional
short journey by rail to visit his relatives, as an obedient
concession to the more insistent but vicarious conscience of his
brother, Colonel John, who was apt to accuse him of neglecting
poor old William's family. Groby usually forgot or ignored
the existence of his neighbour kinsfolk until such time as
he was threatened with a visit from the Colonel, when he
would put matters straight by a hurried pilgrimage across the
few miles of intervening country to renew his acquaintance
with the young people and assume a kindly if rather forced
interest in the well-being of his sister-in-law. On this occasion
he had cut matters so fine between the timing of his exculpatory
visit and the coming of Colonel John, that he would scarcely
be home before the latter was due to arrive. Anyhow, Groby
had got it over, and six or seven months might decently elapse
before he need again sacrifice his comforts and inclinations

on the altar of family sociability. He was inclined to be distinctly cheerful as he hopped about the room, picking up first one object, then another, and subjecting each to a brief bird-like scrutiny.

Presently his cheerful listlessness changed sharply to an attitude of vexed attention. In a scrap-book of drawings and caricatures belonging to one of his nephews he had come across an unkindly clever sketch of himself and his parrot, solemnly confronting each other in postures of ridiculous gravity and repose, and bearing a likeness to one another that the artist had done his utmost to accentuate. After the first flush of annoyance had passed away, Groby laughed good-naturedly and admitted to himself the cleverness of the drawing. Then the feeling of resentment repossessed him, resentment not against the caricaturist who had embodied the idea in pen and ink, but against the possible truth that the idea represented. Was it really the case that people grew in time to resemble the animals they kept as pets, and had he unconsciously become more and more like the comically solemn bird that was his constant companion? Groby was unusually silent as he walked to the train with his escort of chattering nephews and nieces, and during the short railway journey his mind was more and more possessed with an introspective conviction that he had gradually settled down into a sort of parrot-like existence. What, after all, did his daily routine amount to but a sedate meandering and pecking and perching, in his garden, among his fruit trees, in his wicker chair on the lawn, or by the fireside in his library? And what was the sum total of his conversation with chance-encountered neighbours? 'Quite a spring day, isn't it?' 'It looks as though we should have some rain.' 'Glad to see you about again; you must take care of yourself.' 'How the young folk shoot up, don't they?' Strings of stupid, inevitable perfunctory remarks came to his mind, remarks that were certainly not the mental exchange of human intelligences, but mere empty parrot-talk. One might really just as well salute one's acquaintances with 'Pretty polly. Puss, puss, miaow!' Groby began to fume against the picture of himself as a foolish feathered fowl which his nephew's sketch had first suggested, and which his own accusing imagination was filling in with such unflattering detail.

'I'll give the beastly bird away,' he said resentfully; though he knew at the same time that he would do no such thing. It would look so absurd after all the years that he had kept the parrot and made much of it suddenly to try and find it a new home.

'Has my brother arrived?' he asked of the stable-boy, who had come with the pony-carriage to meet him.

'Yessir, came down by the two-fifteen. Your parrot's dead.' The boy made the latter announcement with the relish which his class finds in proclaiming a catastrophe.

'My parrot dead?' said Groby. 'What caused its death?'

'The ipe,' said the boy briefly.

'The ipe?' queried Groby. 'Whatever's that?'

'The ipe what the Colonel brought down with him,' came the rather alarming answer.

'Do you mean to say my brother is ill?' asked Groby. 'Is it something infectious?'

'Th' Colonel's so well as ever he was,' said the boy; and as no further explanation was forthcoming Groby had to possess himself in mystified patience till he reached home. His brother was waiting for him at the hall door.

'Have you heard about the parrot?' he asked at once. ''Pon my soul I'm awfully sorry. The moment he saw the monkey I'd brought down as a surprise for you he squawked out "Rats to you, sir!" and the blessed monkey made one spring at him, got him by the neck and whirled him round like a rattle. He was as dead as mutton by the time I'd got him out of the little beggar's paws. Always been such a friendly little beast, the monkey has, should never have thought he'd got it in him to see red like that. Can't tell you how sorry I feel about it, and now of course you'll hate the sight of the monkey.'

' Not at all,' said Groby sincerely.   A few hours earlier the tragic end which had befallen his parrot would have presented itself to him as a calamity; now it arrived almost as a polite attention on the part of the Fates.

' The bird was getting old, you know,' he went on, in explanation of his obvious lack of decent regret at the loss of his pet. ' I was really beginning to wonder if it was an unmixed kindness to let him go on living till he succumbed to old age.   What a charming little monkey! ' he added, when he was introduced to the culprit.

The newcomer was a small, long-tailed monkey from the Western Hemisphere, with a gentle, half-shy, half-trusting manner that instantly captured Groby's confidence; a student of simian character might have seen in the fitful red light in its eyes some indication of the underlying temper which the parrot had so rashly put to the test with such dramatic consequences for itself.   The servants, who had come to regard the defunct bird as a regular member of the household, and one who gave really very little trouble, were scandalized to find his bloodthirsty aggressor installed in his place as an honoured domestic pet.

' A nasty heathen ipe what don't never say nothing sensible and cheerful, same as pore Polly did,' was the unfavourable verdict of the kitchen quarters.

. . .

One Sunday morning, some twelve or fourteen months after the visit of Colonel John and the parrot-tragedy, Miss Wepley sat decorously in her pew in the parish church, immediately in front of that occupied by Groby Lington.   She was, comparatively speaking, a new-comer in the neighbourhood, and was not personally acquainted with her fellow-worshipper in the seat behind, but for the past two years the Sunday morning service had brought them regularly within each other's sphere of consciousness.   Without having paid particular attention to the subject, she could probably have given a correct rendering of the way in which he pronounced certain words occurring in the responses, while he was well aware of the trivial fact that, in addition to her prayer book and handkerchief, a small paper packet of throat lozenges always reposed on the seat beside her. Miss Wepley rarely had recourse to her lozenges, but in case she should be taken with a fit of coughing she wished to have the emergency duly provided for. On this particular Sunday the lozenges occasioned an unusual diversion in the even tenor of her devotions, far more disturbing to her personally than a prolonged attack of coughing would have been. As she rose to take part in the singing of the first hymn, she fancied that she saw the hand of her neighbour, who was alone in the pew behind her, make a furtive downward grab at the packet lying on the seat; on turning sharply round she found that the packet had certainly disappeared, but Mr. Lington was to all outward seeming serenely intent on his hymn-book. No amount of interrogatory glaring on the part of the despoiled lady could bring the least shade of conscious guilt to his face.

'Worse was to follow,' as she remarked afterwards to a scandalized audience of friends and acquaintances. 'I had scarcely knelt in prayer when a lozenge, one of *my* lozenges, came whizzing into the pew, just under my nose. I turned round and stared, but Mr. Lington had his eyes closed and his lips moving as though engaged in prayer. The moment I resumed my devotions another lozenge came rattling in, and then another. I took no notice for awhile, and then turned round suddenly just as the dreadful man was about to flip another one at me. He hastily pretended to be turning over the leaves of his book, but I was not to be taken in that time. He saw that he had been discovered and no more lozenges came. Of course I have changed my pew.'

'No gentleman would have acted in such a disgraceful manner,' said one of her listeners; 'and yet Mr. Lington used to be so respected by everybody. He seems to have behaved like a little ill-bred schoolboy.'

'He behaved like a monkey,' said Miss Wepley.

Her unfavourable verdict was echoed in other quarters about the same time. Groby Lington had never been a hero in the eyes of his personal retainers, but he had shared the approval accorded to his defunct parrot as a cheerful, well-dispositioned body, who gave no particular trouble. Of late months, however, this character would hardly have been endorsed by the members of his domestic establishment. The stolid stable-boy, who had first announced to him the tragic end of his feathered pet, was one of the first to give voice to the murmurs of disapproval which became rampant and general in the servants' quarters, and he had fairly substantial grounds for his disaffection. In a burst of hot summer weather he had obtained permission to bathe in a modest-sized pond in the orchard, and thither one afternoon Groby had bent his steps, attracted by loud imprecations of anger mingled with the shriller chattering of monkey-language. He beheld his plump diminutive servitor, clad only in a waistcoat and a pair of socks, storming ineffectually at the monkey which was seated on a low branch of an apple tree, abstractedly fingering the remainder of the boy's outfit, which he had removed just out of his reach.

'The ipe's been an' took my clothes,' whined the boy, with the passion of his kind for explaining the obvious. His incomplete toilet effect rather embarrassed him, but he hailed the arrival of Groby with relief, as promising moral and material support in his efforts to get back his raided garments. The monkey had ceased its defiant jabbering, and doubtless with a little coaxing from its master it would hand back the plunder.

'If I lift you up,' suggested Groby, 'you will just be able to reach the clothes.'

The boy agreed, and Groby clutched him firmly by the waistcoat, which was about all there was to catch hold of, and lifted him clear of the ground. Then, with a deft swing he sent him crashing into a clump of tall nettles, which closed receptively round him. The victim had not been brought up in a school which teaches one to repress one's emotions—if a fox had attempted to gnaw at his vitals he would have flown to complain to the nearest hunt committee rather than have affected an attitude of stoical indifference. On this occasion the volume of sound which he produced under the stimulus of pain and rage and astonishment was generous and sustained, but above his bellowings he could distinctly hear the triumphant chattering of his enemy in the tree, and a peal of shrill laughter from Groby.

When the boy had finished an improvised St. Vitus caracole, which would have brought him fame on the boards of the Coliseum, and which indeed met with ready appreciation and applause from the retreating figure of Groby Lington, he found that the monkey had also discreetly retired, while his clothes were scattered on the grass at the foot of the tree.

'They'm two ipes, that's what they be,' he muttered angrily, and if his judgment was severe, at least he spoke under the sting of considerable provocation.

It was a week or two later that the parlour-maid gave notice, having been terrified almost to tears by an outbreak of sudden temper on the part of the master anent some underdone cutlets. ''E gnashed 'is teeth at me, 'e did reely,' she informed a sympathetic kitchen audience.

'I'd like to see 'im talk like that to me, I would,' said the cook defiantly, but her cooking from that moment showed a marked improvement.

It was seldom that Groby Lington so far detached himself from his accustomed habits as to go and form one of a house-party, and he was not a little piqued that Mrs. Glenduff should have stowed him away in the musty old Georgian wing of the house, in the next room, moreover, to Leonard Spabbink, the eminent pianist.

'He plays Liszt like an angel,' had been the hostess's enthusiastic testimonial.

'He may play him like a trout for all I care,' had been Groby's mental comment, 'but I wouldn't mind betting that he snores. He's just the sort and shape that would. And if I hear him snoring through those ridiculous thin-panelled walls, there'll be trouble.'

He did, and there was.

Groby stood it for about two and a quarter minutes, and then made his way through the corridor into Spabbink's room. Under Groby's vigorous measures the musician's flabby, redundant figure sat up in bewildered semi-consciousness like an ice-cream that has been taught to beg. Groby prodded him into complete wakefulness, and then the pettish self-satisfied pianist fairly lost his temper and slapped his domineering visitant on the hand. In another moment Spabbink was being nearly stifled and very effectually gagged by a pillow-case tightly bound round his head, while his plump pyjama'd limbs were hauled out of bed and smacked, pinched, kicked, and bumped in a catch-as-catch-can progress across the floor, towards the flat shallow bath in whose utterly inadequate depths Groby perseveringly strove to drown him. For a few moments the room was almost in darkness: Groby's candle had overturned in an early stage of the scuffle, and its flicker scarcely reached to the spot where splashings, smacks, muffled cries, and splutterings, and a chatter of ape-like rage told of the struggle that was being waged round the shores of the bath. A few instants later the one-sided combat was brightly lit up by the flare of blazing curtains and rapidly kindling panelling.

When the hastily aroused members of the house-party stampeded out on to the lawn, the Georgian wing was well alight and belching forth masses of smoke, but some moments elapsed before Groby appeared with the half-drowned pianist in his arms, having just bethought him of the superior drowning facilities offered by the pond at the bottom of the lawn. The cool night air sobered his rage, and when he found that he was innocently acclaimed as the heroic rescuer of poor Leonard Spabbink, and loudly commended for his presence of mind in tying a wet cloth round his head to protect him from smoke suffocation, he accepted the situation, and subsequently gave a graphic account of his finding the musician asleep with an overturned candle by his side and the conflagration well started. Spabbink gave *his* version some days later, when he had partially recovered from the shock of his midnight castigation and immersion, but the gentle pitying smiles and evasive comments with which his story was greeted warned him that the public ear was not at his disposal. He refused, however, to attend the ceremonial presentation of the Royal Humane Society's life-saving medal.

It was about this time that Groby's pet monkey fell a victim to the disease which attacks so many of its kind when brought under the influence of a northern climate. Its master appeared to be profoundly affected by its loss, and never quite recovered the level of spirits that he had recently attained. In company with the tortoise, which Colonel John presented to him on his last visit, he potters about his lawn and kitchen garden, with none of his erstwhile sprightliness; and his nephews and nieces are fairly well justified in alluding to him as 'Old Uncle Groby.'

FOR THE BEST IN PAPERBACKS, LOOK FOR THE 🐧

In every corner of the world, on every subject under the sun, Penguin represents quality and variety – the very best in publishing today.

For complete information about books available from Penguin – including Pelicans, Puffins, Peregrines and Penguin Classics – and how to order them, write to us at the appropriate address below. Please note that for copyright reasons the selection of books varies from country to country.

In the United Kingdom: Please write to *Dept E.P., Penguin Books Ltd, Harmondsworth, Middlesex, UB7 0DA*

If you have any difficulty in obtaining a title, please send your order with the correct money, plus ten per cent for postage and packaging, to *PO Box No 11, West Drayton, Middlesex*

In the United States: Please write to *Dept BA, Penguin, 299 Murray Hill Parkway, East Rutherford, New Jersey 07073*

In Canada: Please write to *Penguin Books Canada Ltd, 2801 John Street, Markham, Ontario L3R 1B4*

In Australia: Please write to the *Marketing Department, Penguin Books Australia Ltd, P.O. Box 257, Ringwood, Victoria 3134*

In New Zealand: Please write to the *Marketing Department, Penguin Books (NZ) Ltd, Private Bag, Takapuna, Auckland 9*

In India: Please write to *Penguin Overseas Ltd, 706 Eros Apartments, 56 Nehru Place, New Delhi, 110019*

In Holland: Please write to *Penguin Books Nederland B.V., Postbus 195, NL–1380AD Weesp, Netherlands*

In Germany: Please write to *Penguin Books Ltd, Friedrichstrasse 10–12, D–6000 Frankfurt Main 1, Federal Republic of Germany*

In Spain: Please write to *Longman Penguin España, Calle San Nicolas 15, E–28013 Madrid, Spain*

In France: Please write to *Penguin Books Ltd, 39 Rue de Montmorency, F-75003, Paris, France*

In Japan: Please write to *Longman Penguin Japan Co Ltd, Yamaguchi Building, 2–12–9 Kanda Jimbocho, Chiyoda-Ku, Tokyo 101, Japan*

FOR THE BEST IN PAPERBACKS, LOOK FOR THE 🐧

CLASSICS OF THE TWENTIETH CENTURY

The Collected Stories of Elizabeth Bowen

Seventy-nine stories – love stories, ghost stories, stories of childhood and of London during the Blitz – which all prove that 'the instinctive artist is there at the very heart of her work' – Angus Wilson

Look Homeward, Angel   Thomas Wolfe

A lonely idealist in pursuit of 'the great forgotten language, the lost lane-end into heaven', Eugene Gant, the central figure in Wolfe's account of a young boy growing to manhood, scours literature and the world for fresh wonders, until confronted by the intransigent reality of death and disease.

Chéri and The Last of Chéri   Colette

Two novels that 'form the classic analysis of a love-affair between a very young man and a middle-aged woman' – Raymond Mortimer

Selected Poems 1923–1967   Jorge Luis Borges

A magnificent bilingual edition of the poetry of one of the greatest writers of today, conjuring up a unique world of invisible roses, uncaught tigers . . .

Beware of Pity   Stefan Zweig

A cavalry officer becomes involved in the suffering of a young girl; when he attempts to avoid the consequences of his behaviour, the results prove fatal . . .

Valmouth and Other Novels   Ronald Firbank

The world of Ronald Firbank – vibrant, colourful and fantastic – is to be found beneath soft deeps of velvet sky dotted with cognac clouds.

FOR THE BEST IN PAPERBACKS, LOOK FOR THE 🐧

CLASSICS OF THE TWENTIETH CENTURY

Death of a Salesman Arthur Miller

One of the great American plays of the century, this classic study of failure brings to life an unforgettable character: Willy Loman, the shifting and inarticulate hero who is nonetheless a unique individual.

The Echoing Grove Rosamund Lehmann

'No English writer has told of the pains of women in love more truly or more movingly than Rosamund Lehmann' – Marghenita Laski. 'This novel is one of the most absorbing I have read for years' – Simon Raven, in the *Listener*

Pale Fire Vladimir Nabokov

This book contains the last poem by John Shade, together with a Preface, notes and Index by his posthumous editor. But is the eccentric editor more than just haughty and intolerant – mad, bad, perhaps even dangerous . . .?

The Man Who Was Thursday G. K. Chesterton

This hilarious extravaganza concerns a secret society of revolutionaries sworn to destroy the world. But when Thursday turns out to be not a poet but a Scotland Yard detective, one starts to wonder about the identity of the others . . .

The Rebel Albert Camus

Camus's attempt to understand 'the time I live in' tries to justify innocence in an age of atrocity. 'One of the vital works of our time, compassionate and disillusioned, intelligent but instructed by deeply felt experience' – *Observer*

Letters to Milena Franz Kafka

Perhaps the greatest collection of love letters written in the twentieth century, they are an orgy of bliss and despair, of ecstasy and desperation poured out by Kafka in his brief two-year relationship with Milena Jesenska.

FOR THE BEST IN PAPERBACKS, LOOK FOR THE 🐧

CLASSICS OF THE TWENTIETH CENTURY

The Age of Reason   Jean-Paul Sartre

The first part of Sartre's classic trilogy, set in the volatile Paris summer of 1938, is itself 'a dynamic, deeply disturbing novel' (Elizabeth Bowen) which tackles some of the major issues of our time.

Three Lives   Gertrude Stein

A turning point in American literature, these portraits of three women – thin, worn Anna, patient, gentle Lena and the complicated, intelligent Melanctha – represented in 1909 one of the pioneering examples of modernist writing.

Doctor Faustus   Thomas Mann

Perhaps the most convincing description of an artistic genius ever written, this portrait of the composer Leverkuhn is a classic statement of one of Mann's obsessive themes: the discord between genius and sanity.

The New Machiavelli   H. G. Wells

This autobiography of a man who has thrown up a glittering political career and marriage to go into exile with the woman he loves also contains an illuminating Introduction by Melvyn Bragg.

The Collected Poems of Stevie Smith

Amused, amusing and deliciously barbed, this volume includes many poems which dwell on death; as a whole, though, as this first complete edition in paperback makes clear, Smith's poetry affirms an irrepressible love of life.

Rhinoceros / The Chairs / The Lesson   Eugène Ionesco

Three great plays by the man who was one of the founders of what has come to be known as the Theatre of the Absurd.

The Second Sex   Simone de Beauvoir

This great study of Woman is a landmark in feminist history, drawing together insights from biology, history and sociology as well as literature, psychoanalysis and mythology to produce one of the supreme classics of the twentieth century.

The Bridge of San Luis Rey   Thornton Wilder

On 20 July 1714 the finest bridge in all Peru collapsed, killing 5 people. Why? Did it reveal a latent pattern in human life? In this beautiful, vivid and compassionate investigation, Wilder asks some searching questions in telling the story of the survivors.

Parents and Children   Ivy Compton-Burnett

This richly entertaining introduction to the world of a unique novelist brings to light the deadly claustrophobia within a late-Victorian upper-middle-class family . . .

We   Yevgeny Zamyatin

Zamyatin's nightmarish vision of the future is both a masterpiece in its own right and the forerunner of Huxley's *Brave New World* and Orwell's *1984*. The story of D-503, who is aroused from acceptance of the totalitarian state by a strange woman, E-330. His revolution is vividly chronicled here in his diary.

Confessions of Zeno   Italo Svevo

Zeno, an innocent in a corrupt world, triumphs in the end through his stoic acceptance of his own failings in this extraordinary, experimental novel that fuses memory, obsession and desire.

Southern Mail/Night Flight   Antoine de Saint-Exupéry

Both novels in this volume are concerned with the pilot's solitary struggle with the elements, his sensation of insignificance amidst the stars' timelessness and the sky's immensity. Flying and writing were inextricably linked in the author's life and he brought a unique sense of dedication to both.

CLASSICS OF THE TWENTIETH CENTURY

Gertrude   Hermann Hesse

A sensitive young composer, the narrator is drawn to Gertrude through their mutual love of music. Gradually, he is engulfed by an enduring and hopeless passion for her. 'It would be a pity to miss this book – it has such a rare flavour of truth and simplicity' – Stevie Smith in the *Observer*

If It Die   André Gide

A masterpiece of French prose, *If It Die* is Gide's record of his childhood, his friendships, his travels, his sexual awakening and, above all, the search for truth which characterizes his whole life and all his writing.

Dark as the Grave wherein my Friend is Laid   Malcolm Lowry

A Dantean descent into hell, into the infernal landscape of Mexico, the same Mexico as Lowry's *Under the Volcano*, a country of mental terrors and spiritual chasms.

The Collected Short Stories   Katherine Mansfield

'She could discern in a trivial event or an insignificant person some moving revelation or motive or destiny . . . There is an abundance of that tender and delicate art which penetrates the appearances of life to discover the elusive causes of happiness and grief' – W. E. Williams in his Introduction to *The Garden Party and Other Stories*

Sanctuary   William Faulkner

Faulkner draws America's Deep South exactly as he saw it: seething with life and corruption; and *Sanctuary* asserts itself as a compulsive and unsparing vision of human nature.

The Expelled and Other Novellas   Samuel Beckett

Rich in verbal and situational humour, the four stories in this volume offer the reader a fascinating insight into Beckett's preoccupation with the helpless individual consciousness, a preoccupation which has remained constant throughout Beckett's work.

A CHOICE OF PENGUIN FICTION

The Power and the Glory   Graham Greene

During an anti-clerical purge in one of the southern states of Mexico, the last priest is hunted like a hare. Too humble for martyrdom, too human for heroism, he is nevertheless impelled towards his squalid Calvary. 'There is no better story-teller in English today' – V. S. Pritchett

The Enigma of Arrival   V. S. Naipaul

'For sheer abundance of talent, there can hardly be a writer alive who surpasses V. S. Naipaul. Whatever we may want in a novelist is to be found in his books . . .' – Irving Howe in *The New York Times Book Review*. 'Naipaul is always brilliant' – Anthony Burgess in the *Observer*

Earthly Powers   Anthony Burgess

Anthony Burgess's magnificent masterpiece, an enthralling, epic narrative spanning six decades and spotlighting some of the most vivid events and characters of our times. 'Enormous imagination and vitality . . . a huge book in every way' – Bernard Levin in the *Sunday Times*

The Penitent   Isaac Bashevis Singer

From the Nobel Prize-winning author comes a powerful story of a man who has material wealth but feels spiritually impoverished. 'Singer . . . restates with dignity the spiritual aspirations and the cultural complexities of a lifetime, and it must be said that in doing so he gives the Evil One no quarter and precious little advantage' – Anita Brookner in the *Sunday Times*

Paradise Postponed   John Mortimer

'Hats off to John Mortimer. He's done it again' – *Spectator*. A rumbustious, hilarious novel from the creator of Rumpole, *Paradise Postponed* examines British life since the war to discover why Paradise has always been postponed.

The Balkan Trilogy and Levant Trilogy   Olivia Manning

'The finest fictional record of the war produced by a British writer. Her gallery of personages is huge, her scene painting superb, her pathos controlled, her humour quiet and civilized' – *Sunday Times*

FOR THE BEST IN PAPERBACKS, LOOK FOR THE 🐧

A CHOICE OF PENGUIN FICTION

Maia Richard Adams

The heroic romance of love and war in an ancient empire from one of our greatest storytellers. 'Enormous and powerful' – *Financial Times*

The Warning Bell Lynne Reid Banks

A wonderfully involving, truthful novel about the choices a woman must make in her life – and the price she must pay for ignoring the counsel of her own heart. 'Lynne Reid Banks knows how to get to her reader: this novel grips like Super Glue' – *Observer*

Doctor Slaughter Paul Theroux

Provocative and menacing – a brilliant dissection of lust, ambition and betrayal in 'civilized' London. 'Witty, chilly, exuberant, graphic' – *The Times Literary Supplement*

Wise Virgin A. N. Wilson

Giles Fox's work on the Pottle manuscript, a little-known thirteenth-century tract on virginity, leads him to some innovative research on the subject that takes even his breath away. 'A most elegant and chilling comedy' – *Observer* Books of the Year

Gone to Soldiers Marge Piercy

Until now, the passions, brutality and devastation of the Second World War have only been written about by men. Here for the first time, one of America's major writers brings a woman's depth and intensity to the panorama of world war. 'A victory' – *Newsweek*

Trade Wind M. M. Kaye

An enthralling blend of history, adventure and romance from the author of the bestselling *The Far Pavilions*

A CHOICE OF PENGUIN FICTION

Stanley and the Women   Kingsley Amis

Just when Stanley Duke thinks it safe to sink into middle age, his son goes insane – and Stanley finds himself beset on all sides by women, each of whom seems to have an intimate acquaintance with madness. 'Very good, very powerful . . . beautifully written' – Anthony Burgess in the *Observer*

The Girls of Slender Means   Muriel Spark

A world and a war are winding up with a bang, and in what is left of London, all the nice people are poor – and about to discover how different the new world will be. 'Britain's finest post-war novelist' – *The Times*

Him with His Foot in His Mouth   Saul Bellow

A collection of first-class short stories. 'If there is a better living writer of fiction, I'd very much like to know who he or she is' – *The Times*

Mother's Helper   Maureen Freely

A superbly biting and breathtakingly fluent attack on certain libertarian views, blending laughter, delight, rage and amazement, this is a novel you won't forget. 'A winner' – *The Times Literary Supplement*

Decline and Fall   Evelyn Waugh

A comic yet curiously touching account of an innocent plunged into the sham, brittle world of high society. Evelyn Waugh's first novel brought him immediate public acclaim and is still a classic of its kind.

Stars and Bars   William Boyd

Well-dressed, quite handsome, unfailingly polite and charming, who would guess that Henderson Dores, the innocent Englishman abroad in wicked America, has a guilty secret? 'Without doubt his best book so far . . . made me laugh out loud' – *The Times*

A CHOICE OF PENGUIN FICTION

The Ghost Writer   Philip Roth

Philip Roth's celebrated novel about a young writer who meets and falls in love with Anne Frank in New England – or so he thinks. 'Brilliant, witty and extremely elegant' – *Guardian*

Small World   David Lodge

Shortlisted for the 1984 Booker Prize, *Small World* brings back Philip Swallow and Maurice Zapp for a jet-propelled journey into hilarity. 'The most brilliant and also the funniest novel that he has written' – *London Review of Books*

Moon Tiger   Penelope Lively

Winner of the 1987 Booker Prize, *Moon Tiger* is Penelope Lively's 'most ambitious book to date' – *The Times* 'A complex tapestry of great subtlety . . . Penelope Lively writes so well, savouring the words as she goes' – *Daily Telegraph* 'A very clever book: it is evocative, thought-provoking and hangs curiously on the edges of the mind long after it is finished' – *Literary Review*

Absolute Beginners   Colin MacInnes

The first 'teenage' novel, the classic of youth and disenchantment, *Absolute Beginners* is part of MacInnes's famous London trilogy – and now a brilliant film. 'MacInnes caught it first – and best' – *Harpers and Queen*

July's People   Nadine Gordimer

Set in South Africa, this novel gives us an unforgettable look at the terrifying, tacit understandings and misunderstandings between blacks and whites. 'This is the best novel that Miss Gordimer has ever written' – Alan Paton in the *Saturday Review*

The Ice Age   Margaret Drabble

'A continuously readable, continuously surprising book . . . here is a novelist who is not only popular and successful but formidably growing towards real stature' – *Observer*

FOR THE BEST IN PAPERBACKS, LOOK FOR THE 🐧

A CHOICE OF PENGUIN FICTION

Money   Martin Amis

Savage, audacious and demonically witty – a story of urban excess. 'Terribly, terminally funny: laughter in the dark, if ever I heard it' – *Guardian*

Lolita   Vladimir Nabokov

Shot through with Nabokov's mercurial wit, quicksilver prose and intoxicating sensuality, *Lolita* is one of the world's greatest love stories. 'A great book' – Dorothy Parker

Dinner at the Homesick Restaurant   Anne Tyler

Through every family run memories that bind them together – in spite of everything. 'She is a witch. Witty, civilized, curious, with her radar ears and her quill pen dipped on one page in acid and on the next in orange liqueur . . . a wonderful writer' – John Leonard in *The New York Times*

Glitz   Elmore Leonard

Underneath the Boardwalk, a lot of insects creep. But the creepiest of all was Teddy. 'After finishing *Glitz*, I went out to the bookstore and bought everything else of Elmore Leonard's I could find' – Stephen King

Trust   Mary Flanagan

Charles was a worthy man – a trustworthy man – a thing rare and old-fashioned in Eleanor's experience. 'A vivid, passionate roller-coaster of a book, which is also expertly crafted and beautifully written' – *Punch* 'A rare and sensitive début novel . . . there is something much more powerful than a moral in this novel – there is acute observation. It stands up to scrutiny. It rings true' – *Fiction Magazine*

The Levels   Peter Benson

Winner of the Guardian Fiction Prize

Set in the secret landscape of the Somerset Levels, this remarkable first novel is the story of a young boy whose first encounter with love both bruises and enlarges his vision of the world. 'It discovers things about life that we recognise with a gasp' – *The Times*

A CHOICE OF PENGUIN FICTION

The Dearest and the Best   Leslie Thomas

In the spring of 1940 the spectre of war turned into grim reality – and for all the inhabitants of the historic villages of the New Forest it was the beginning of the most bizarre, funny and tragic episode of their lives. 'Excellent' – *Sunday Times*

Only Children   Alison Lurie

When the Hubbards and the Zimmerns go to visit Anna on her idyllic farm, it becomes increasingly difficult to tell which are the adults, and which the children. 'It demands to be read' – *Financial Times* 'There quite simply is no better living writer' – John Braine

My Family and Other Animals   Gerald Durrell

Gerald Durrell's wonderfully comic account of his childhood years on Corfu and his development as a naturalist and zoologist is a true delight. Soaked in Greek sunshine, it is a 'bewitching book' – *Sunday Times*

Getting it Right   Elizabeth Jane Howard

A hairdresser in the West End, Gavin is sensitive, shy, into the arts, prone to spots and, at thirty-one, a virgin. He's a classic late developer – and maybe it's getting too late to develop at all? 'Crammed with incidental pleasures . . . sometimes sad but more frequently hilarious . . . *Getting it Right* gets it, comically, right' – Paul Bailey in the *London Standard*

The Vivisector   Patrick White

In this prodigious novel about the life and death of a great painter, Patrick White, winner of the Nobel Prize for Literature, illuminates creative experience with unique truthfulness. 'One of the most interesting and absorbing novelists writing English today' – Angus Wilson in the *Observer*

The Echoing Grove   Rosamund Lehmann

'No English writer has told of the pains of women in love more truly or more movingly than Rosamund Lehmann' – Marghanita Laski. 'She uses words with the enjoyment and mastery with which Renoir used paint' – Rebecca West in the *Sunday Times* 'A magnificent achievement' – John Connell in the *Evening News*

FOR THE BEST IN PAPERBACKS, LOOK FOR THE 🐧

A CHOICE OF PENGUIN FICTION

Other Women Lisa Alther

From the bestselling author of *Kinflicks* comes this compelling novel of today's woman – and a heroine with whom millions of women will identify.

Your Lover Just Called John Updike

Stories of Joan and Richard Maple – a couple multiplied by love and divided by lovers. Here is the portrait of a modern American marriage in all its mundane moments and highs and lows of love as only John Updike could draw it.

Mr Love and Justice Colin MacInnes

Frankie Love took up his career as a ponce at about the same time as Edward Justice became vice-squad detective. Except that neither man was particularly suited for his job, all they had in common was an interest in crime. Provocative and honest and acidly funny, *Mr Love and Justice* is the final volume of Colin MacInnes's famous London trilogy.

An Ice-Cream War William Boyd

As millions are slaughtered on the Western Front, a ridiculous and little-reported campaign is being waged in East Africa – a war they continued after the Armistice because no one told them to stop. 'A towering achievement' – John Carey, Chairman of the Judges of the 1982 Booker Prize, for which this novel was shortlisted.

Fool's Sanctuary Jennifer Johnston

Set in Ireland in the 1920s, Jennifer Johnston's beautiful novel tells of Miranda's growing up into political awareness. Loyalty, romance and friendship are fractured by betrayal and the gunman's flight for freedom, honour and pride. 'Her novels . . . are near perfect literary jewels' – *Cosmopolitan*

The Big Sleep Raymond Chandler

'I was neat, clean, shaved and sober, and I didn't care who knew it. I was everything the well-dressed private detective ought to be. I was calling ~~ four million dollars'. 'A book to be read at a sitting' – *Sunday Times*

A CHOICE OF PENGUIN FICTION

A Fanatic Heart   Edna O'Brien

'A selection of twenty-nine stories (including four new ones) full of wit and feeling and savagery that prove that Edna O'Brien is one of the subtlest and most lavishly gifted writers we have' – A. Alvarez in the *Observer*

Charade   John Mortimer

'Wonderful comedy . . . an almost Firbankian melancholy . . . John Mortimer's hero is helplessly English' – *Punch*. 'What is *Charade*? Comedy? Tragedy? Mystery? It is all three and more' – *Daily Express*

Casualties   Lynne Reid Banks

'The plot grips; the prose is fast-moving and elegant; above all, the characters are wincingly, winningly human . . . if literary prizes were awarded for craftsmanship and emotional directness, *Casualties* would head the field' – *Daily Telegraph*

The Anatomy Lesson   Philip Roth

The hilarious story of Nathan Zuckerman, the famous forty-year-old writer who decides to give it all up and become a doctor – and a pornographer – instead. 'The finest, boldest and funniest piece of fiction that Philip Roth has yet produced' – *Spectator*

Gabriel's Lament   Paul Bailey

Shortlisted for the 1986 Booker Prize
'The best novel yet by one of the most careful fiction craftsmen of his generation' – *Guardian*. 'A magnificent novel, moving, eccentric and unforgettable. He has a rare feeling for language and an understanding of character which few can rival' – *Daily Telegraph*

Small Changes   Marge Piercy

In the Sixties the world seemed to be making big changes – but for many women it was the small changes that were the hardest and the most profound. *Small Changes* is Marge Piercy's explosive new novel about women fighting to make their way in a man's world.